TRUTH & POWER

MEN OF MAGIC BOOK TWO

ADDISON ARROWDELL

Truth & Power: Men of Magic Book Two

Copyright © 2021 by Addison Arrowdell

SECOND EDITION

Copyright © 2022 by Addison Arrowdell

Print ISBN: 978-1-7395899-2-9

ONE

ELBA SMOOTHED her shaking hands over her navy skirt, trying to look as though she wasn't trembling at her very core. Around her, the atrium of the Men of Magic headquarters—or the less conspicuously named 'bureau'—was less busy on a Saturday than it had been just a couple of days before, when she'd been registered.

Despite the reduced staff, a winding queue had formed at the stone security gate, and every second Elba spent in line sent her heart rate creeping up. Risking a glance at Hemingway and Kipling, painfully handsome in their smart, dark suits, she wondered whether they were as nervous as her beneath their cool, calm exteriors.

Sensing her gaze, Kip gave her a reassuring smile before returning his attention to the queue at the security gate. Elba stood close enough to feel his warmth and it took all her self-control not to wrap her arms around him or slip her hand into his. This was the longest they'd not had physical contact since they'd finally admitted how they felt about each other the morning before. It was probably the longest she'd worn clothes since then, too. Elba's cheeks warmed as her mind

1

conjured images of his chiselled body, glistening with sweat, her name on his lips. She swallowed.

"We could totally push to the front," Hem grumbled, tucking a strand of golden hair behind his ear. "We outrank every single one of these fuckers."

In front of them, an older man wearing a sharp pinstripe suit turned and glared up at him.

"You all right, Norman?" Hem winked.

Elba pressed her lips together to hold in her laugh. It was only the second time she'd visited the bureau. The last time she'd been here, she'd been registered. All Normals who discovered magic and abstained from having their memory wiped had to be registered. At the time it had made sense, but since the discovery of the magic restrictors implanted in Kipling and Hemingway as children, Elba couldn't help but wonder if the bureau's motives were more sinister.

Her heart drummed a steady rhythm beneath her blouse and jacket as she stared up at the towering stone arch engraved with ancient symbols. What exactly did it detect? Would it be able to tell that she'd wielded magic just two days ago? The man monitoring the gate was the same white-moustached man who'd ushered her through the first time and, as they took a step closer, she wiped her sweaty palms on her skirt again.

"Relax," Kip whispered. "You look like you're about to rob a bank."

Elba tried to glare at him, but she barely managed a scowl before melting into a smile at the gentle laughter glimmering in his silver eyes. Staring down at the polished marble floor, she wondered how far beneath them Selena was being held captive. Was she okay? Even though she'd stood by and watched Kip cut to shreds by Naomi, there was a part of her that had tried to do the right thing, and Elba couldn't help but hope it meant Selena wasn't a lost cause. Perhaps thinking of her as such made it easier for Hemingway to separate her from the woman who'd been the love of his life. Maybe that was why he was reluctant to accept that she might not be as evil as they'd been led to believe. As all Magics had been told Freedoms were.

"Long time no see."

Elba looked up to find a tall woman in a beautifully cut slate-grey suit standing beside them. Her legs seemed to go on forever and her chestnut hair hung in loose waves to her waist. She looked like a model pretending to be a business-woman. Her golden eyes flickered over Elba, a small polite smile on her lips, before turning full beam to the men beside her.

"Bryony." Hem nodded. "It's been a while. How was Scotland?"

"Cold." Bryony tossed her hair over her shoulder. "How are you two? Still the perpetual thorn in the bureau's side?"

Hem chuckled and shrugged his broad shoulders. "I have no idea what you mean."

Elba watched the exchange in seven shades of awkward. She wasn't expecting to be introduced—after all, the fewer Men of Magic who knew who she was the better—but lingering there beside them like a spare part made her insides shrivel. Besides, as far as Kipling and Hemingway were concerned, she shouldn't even be there. She'd had to beg them to let her to come, winning only after pointing out that if it wasn't safe for her, then none of them should be going at all.

"What about you, Kipling? What's new?" Bryony asked, her voice softening an octave as her eyes unabashedly ran the length of him.

Kip gave her an easy smile that didn't quite reach his eyes. "You know. Same old. When did you get back?"

"They ended my secondment early. Something's going on, but they haven't briefed me yet." She leaned a little closer, her gilded eyes looking around before whispering. "I heard a rumour that they're pulling in all the Men."

Kip tensed. "Really?"

"Like I said, just a rumour." Bryony shrugged. "I thought maybe you'd know more."

Hem shoved his hands in his pockets, peering ahead to the front of the queue as though checking what was taking so long. "No. There's a briefing later this week. Maybe they're waiting for everyone to get here first."

"Perhaps." Bryony pressed her lips together before returning her attention to Kipling. She reached across Elba, trailing a perfectly manicured finger down his bicep. "If you fancy a drink—or something more hands on—my number hasn't changed."

"He's busy." The words left Elba's mouth before she'd even realised, her jaw as tightly clenched as her fists.

Kip's eyebrows raised and he opened his mouth to respond, but Bryony swished her hair over her shoulder, her nose wrinkling in disgust. "I think Kipling is more than capable of speaking for himself."

Elba's stomach rolled. What was she doing? Yes, they'd spent the last twenty-four hours naked, but that didn't mean they were a couple. She'd just potentially cock-blocked him from a gorgeous ex, or even worse, perhaps she'd pushed him into her bed. Elba couldn't bring herself to look at him.

"Well, you're both right," Kip said, his voice low with barely concealed amusement. "Yes, Bryony. I can speak for myself, but Elba's also right. I am busy. I'm sure we'll see you at the briefing."

Bryony's plump pink mouth fell open for a moment before snapping shut. She spun on her patent heels, clacking away across the echoing foyer.

Elba blew out a slow breath, her gaze fixed on the floor. "Shit. Sorry."

Hem tried to hide a low chuckle with a cough, causing

4

Elba's cheeks to flame further. She smelt Kip's magic before she felt it—the soft scent of sea salt and citrus—a gentle caress around her lower back, as though an invisible arm was curling around her. Steeling herself, she looked up at him.

Kip smiled down at her, his silver eyes flashing with a mix of amusement and arousal that caused her chest to tighten. He opened his mouth to speak, but before he could utter a word, they found themselves at the front of the gate.

"Hello again." The guard smiled at them.

Hem nodded, sliding his two phones and wallet into the small tray. "Morning, Carl. What's with the queue today?"

The silver-haired guard frowned. "Extra security. They added new wards last night."

A fresh wave of panic rippled through Elba and she felt Kip tense beside her. Did it have anything to do with what had happened at the warehouse?

"Why?" Kip asked as Hem stepped through the archway, causing it to glow a faint blue colour.

Carl shook his head. "The top floor doesn't tell me anything, you know that. No one gets in until the arch deems them safe. Don't ask me how it knows. This new ward is unlike anything I've seen before."

Even as they watched, the archway shimmered, glowing white before returning to its dull grey colour. Carl gave Hem a nod, handing him back his belongings.

"You next," Kip said, shooting her a smile before sharing a look with Hem.

Elba swallowed and pasted a smile on her face as she fished her mobile phone and keys from her pocket. She hadn't bothered bringing a bag, knowing that Kip could magic her anything if she needed it. To be honest, she probably didn't even need her keys.

She stepped through the arch, shuddering at the feeling of a thousand ghostly fingers running over her. It was more intense than before, as though the magic was sorting through the very fibres of her being. What it was searching for, Elba could only guess. The scars on her right breast left by the conduit stone burned hot as the magic settled around her, and she forced herself to breathe as she stepped out from under the arch.

Hem gave her a smile and Elba tried not to feel too unnerved at how serious he looked as he watched the colour of the archway glowing blue. Blood roaring in her ears, she watched the stone, wondering what would happen if it didn't glow white. Would she be carted off to the same holding rooms as Selena? Would she be tortured? What if the conduit stone's symbols triggered something in the new ward?

Elba met Kip's gaze on the other side of the towering stone archway. He didn't smile, but she could see the reassurance in his eyes. Whatever happened, they would go down swinging. Perhaps that's why he'd waited until last, so she was between them.

When the archway flickered to a white glow, it took everything Elba had not to sag to her knees with relief. She collected her things, smiling at the guard as Kipling stepped through. After it glowed white, they bid Carl farewell and headed to the bank of elevators lining the far wall of the lobby.

"That was intense," Elba breathed as the doors pinged closed and Hemingway pressed the button for the twelfth floor.

He turned and grinned at her, his dark blue eyes sparkling as he leaned against the elevator wall. "The new creepy security measures or you baring your teeth at Bryony Baker?"

Elba cringed, turning to look apologetically at Kip. She found him watching her with such intensity that she took a half step back. She opened her mouth to utter the excuses she'd been crafting since Bryony had stalked away from them, but before she could utter a word, Kip muttered a string of strange words that sent a black fog circling the ceiling of the elevator.

Wide-eyed, Elba watched as Kip stalked towards her, sliding one arm around her waist, the other bracing against the wall of the elevator as he claimed her mouth with his. She pressed her body against him, sliding her hands under his suit jacket to trace the lines of muscle beneath his shirt. As the kiss deepened, he pushed against her, making sure she could feel just how much he wanted her. Elba couldn't hold in the small moan against Kip's tongue and she felt his hand tighten around her waist, the air heavy with want around them.

The elevator slowed, a loud ping signalling their arrival at the twelfth floor and Kip stepped back—his breathing unsteady. Elba stared up at him, every fibre of her being calling for her to touch him. There was too much space between them.

"Thank fuck for that," Hem muttered as the doors pinged open and he stepped out into the hallway, his eyes fixed on his phone.

Kip stepped back further, adjusting himself as he nodded for Elba to follow after Hem. Every inch of her was on fire as she walked down the empty corridor. Kip's strides behind her sent tingles down her body, and she bit down on her lip, trying to focus on the golden plaques gleaming uniformly on the rows of black doors.

"Where's your office, Hem?" Elba mused.

"Next door to Kip's," Hem answered, shooting a glance over his shoulder at him. "We can use my office instead if you want."

Kip snorted and Elba narrowed her eyes, looking between the two of them.

"Are you sure?" Kip asked as they walked past his office to come to a halt one door down.

Hem rolled his eyes as he opened the door. "It's not that bad."

Elba stepped inside the office, her eyes widening in shock. She'd been in Hem's apartment several times and it was immaculate—a black and white bachelor pad with zero personality. His office, however, was a completely different story. Her mouth hung open as she took in the framed band posters on the walls, the shelves full of magazines and the desk completely covered with papers and folders. The wastebasket below the desk was filled with food wrappers and several empty coffee take out cups. The layout was identical to Kipling's office, yet it couldn't have been more different. Even the black leather couch was covered with a chunky mustard colour throw that looked well worn.

"I spend a lot of time here," Hem said, folding his arms across his broad chest, "so I like to be comfortable."

Elba nodded, her eyes still taking in the details. "I can see that."

"Go on." Hem sighed. "Out with it."

Elba turned to him. "What?"

"Take the piss out of me."

"Why would I do that?" she said. "I love it. It's like I'm finally getting to see the real you."

"He literally took his half of our shared room from the boarding house and moved it here instead of his apartment," Kip said, wrinkling his nose as he swiped an empty packet of crisps into the trash.

Elba smiled, reaching out to squeeze Hem's tensed forearm as she continued to take in as much of the space as she could. Perhaps she was thinking about it too deeply, but she couldn't understand why his space at work would be so personal when his home was so bare. Was it like this so the women he brought back to the apartment didn't get too close? That said, the bureau was their home. Maybe that was why. If that was the case, why was Kip's office so empty? She hadn't seen his apartment yet. Was that where all his things were?

"Okay," Hem said. "Enough gawking. I'm making the decision for us. We're using Kip's office."

As he ushered them out, Elba couldn't help but grin. He'd let her see a secret part of him she was sure not many people got to see, and the thought warmed her heart.

TWO

KIP OPENED the door to his office and Elba's stomach somersaulted at the familiar space, recalling the way her and Kip had exchanged such harsh words by the window. Her gaze fell on the large glass desk before it and her breath hitched. Memories of being pressed naked against the cool surface, hands tied, as Kip slammed into her until she screamed his name caused her knees to weaken.

Swallowing hard, Elba turned to find Kip staring at her, his silver eyes sparking, a small smile on his lips. Her cheeks flamed as she looked away.

"Do you know what time the interrogation is supposed to start?" Elba asked, sinking down onto the black leather sofa in an attempt to hide her trembling limbs.

Hem frowned, glancing at his watch. "It should be within the next hour according to Eli."

"Are you sure we can trust him?" Kip asked, leaning against the desk.

"If management find out that we're watching a hacked feed, it's Eli that'll get in trouble, not us," Hem reasoned.

Elba crossed her legs, trying not to notice the way Kip's gaze followed the motion, lingering. "Why is he helping us?"

"We joined the bureau at the same time," Hem said. "We've worked together loads over the years. We're not close friends, but we get on. He has no reason to deny me a favour."

"It makes sense that he'd ask, too," Kip added. "Even if things aren't exactly amicable between Hem and Selena, I don't think anyone would be surprised that he'd want to know what was going on."

Elba chewed her lip as she considered the fact. With what she knew about the bureau, it was easy to assume that everyone and everything within its walls was sinister. She tried to imagine the gorgeous red-headed siblings at Christmas parties and after work drinks over the years with the guys. They were right. It wasn't a weird thing to ask. It was their reasons for wanting it that made her so nervous.

Hem strode over to the window, frowning out at the view. Elba wondered how he was feeling, knowing that Selena was being held somewhere far beneath them. She knew they'd been together for a couple of years, so he must have loved her, right?

A light touch ran up the side of her calf and she jolted, glancing down to find nothing there. Before Elba could wonder whether she'd imagined it, the sensation repeated, this time, stroking further up her leg to her thigh. Her eyes flicked to Kip, to find him watching her intently, a faint silver shimmer playing around the fingers on his right hand. As she held his gaze, the touch stroked up the inside of her thigh and she gasped.

Hem shot her a strange look from where he was standing at the window and she forced a smile.

"Do they record all the interrogations?" she asked, ignoring Kip's raised eyebrow.

"I guess so," Hem said. "Eli is pretty sure he can hack it so we can watch from my laptop. He said he'll send a text when he's found the feed."

11

Elba was glad Hem's attention was on the view as she tried to keep the blush from her cheeks. Kip licked his lips as he repeated the movement, this time trailing the touch between her legs. Elba dug her fingers into the soft leather, her breathing quickening as the strokes intensified.

"Why can I smell your magic?" Hem asked, wrinkling his nose as he turned away from the window, pulling out his phone.

Elba's cheeks burned as he glanced between the two of them.

"Seriously?" Hem shook his head as he tapped at the screen. "Eli's just messaged anyway. You've got about fifteen minutes. Don't forget to lock the door."

With a wink, Hem pocked his phone and left, shutting the door behind him. Kip flicked a hand at the closed door, muttering something Elba was fairly certain was to make sure it stayed that way.

Kip kept his eyes on her, his voice little more than a growl. "Come here."

Elba stood on shaking legs and crossed the office to stand in front of him. His hands reached for her waist, pulling her between his legs as his mouth claimed hers. Melting beneath his touch, she slid her hands up his chest, her thumbs stroking his jaw before her fingers tangled in his hair.

"I'm going to have to buy a new desk," he murmured against her neck as he trailed kisses along the sensitive flesh.

Elba closed her eyes, tipping her head back as she gently pulled his shirt from his pants, her fingers craving the warm skin beneath. "Why? It's a nice desk."

"Because," he murmured, his lips against her earlobe, "how am I supposed to get any work done when all I can think about is you bent over it?"

Elba smiled, meeting his darkened stare before trailing kisses along his sharp jaw. The sigh of pleasure the action drew from him caused her chest to contract, heat jolting through her core and pooling between her thighs.

"You are a distraction, Elba," he rumbled, his fingers finding their way under her shirt, encircling her waist.

As his mouth found hers once more, she tried to lose herself in his touch as his fingers began to explore her body, but one thought kept pushing its way to the forefront of her mind. How many other women had been fucked over that desk? It shouldn't matter. She knew there was a line a mile long of women who had come—literally—before her, but she was the one here with him now.

"Where are you?"

Elba blinked, realising Kip was staring at her, a slight frown on his beautiful face. "Sorry. I just got in my own head."

"What's wrong?"

"Nothing." She shook her head and tried to pull his mouth to hers, but he leaned back out of her reach.

Kip fixed her with his silver eyes, his hands on her hips. "Talk to me. Please. There's nothing you can't tell me."

"Seriously," Elba insisted. "It's nothing."

Kip raised a dark eyebrow. "If it's enough to make you space out when I'm taking your clothes off, I want to know."

Looking down, Elba realised with surprise that her shirt was completely unbuttoned, her pale pink bra exposed. She hadn't even noticed. *Shit.*

"I didn't want to have to do this," Kip said, taking her hand in his, "but if you don't tell me . . ." He placed her hand on the erection straining against his pants. "I'm withholding this."

Elba tried to roll her eyes, but at the feel of the thick, hard length beneath her palm, she couldn't help the small intake of breath at the memory of him inside her.

"If I tell you, it's probably going to make that go away," she admitted.

Kip released her hand, lifting his own to her face. "Elba."

A resigned sigh escaped her lips and she raised her eyes to the ceiling. "Fine. Whatever. I was wondering whether you'd bent Bryony over this desk and then I started thinking about how many others there have been as well." She forced herself to look at him. "See. I told you."

Kip shook his head, a sad smile on his lips. "Elba—"

"No," Elba interrupted. "I refuse to be that girl. You don't have to justify or make me feel better. I don't care how many women you've been with. Maybe what happened with Alex has made me a little more insecure than I realised, but I'm not going to put that on you. Can we just forget this, please?"

Kip leaned forward and brushed his lips against hers, before taking her face in his hands once more. "Fine. We can forget it. But I meant what I said in the lobby, about you being right. I am busy. Busy with you. For as long as you want me."

Elba's cheeks heated as she met his silver stare, his gaze intense enough it caused her to look away, turning her attention to his lips instead.

"Ever since I saw you in that alley," he continued, trailing a finger along her cheek and across her lips, "I haven't been able to stop thinking about you. No one has ever filled my head as much as you, Elba. All I can think about is touching you, tasting you, being inside you."

Elba's breath hitched as he pressed a kiss to her lips, his hands moving down her arms then encircling her waist. "Hem will be back any minute."

"Let's not waste any more time, then," Kip said, murmuring the now familiar string of words that caused their clothes to vanish.

Elba gasped at their sudden nakedness, acutely aware of the long rectangle of window that ran the length of the office. Kipling turned her around, lifting her onto his desk as his tongue claimed hers, his fingers dipping between her legs. He moaned against her mouth at the wetness he found there, slipping his fingers inside. Elba's head span, her body alight as she rocked against his hand. Wrapping her legs around him, Kip pumped his fingers inside her, his thumb pressing against her clit.

With a low growl, Kip pulled her forward, pushing his hard length into her in a fluid motion that drew a long moan of pleasure from her lips. His hands sliding to her waist, he lay her down on the desk, his fingers splayed against her stomach. Elba gasped as he thrust into her, gripping her hips with his strong hands. His silver eyes were dark as he drank her in, his magic flickering across her body, intoxicating her with its scent. When she took her own breasts in her hands, Kip swore under his breath, his fingers digging into her skin as he slammed into her harder.

Elba felt her release building and arched her back as the edges of her visioned darkened with pleasure. She opened her eyes in time to see Kip throwing his head back, her name on his lips as a pale shimmer of silver and gold rippled from his sculpted torso.

As her body absorbed the ripples of pleasure, Elba watched, revelling in the sight of him. A chiselled god of silver moonlight and ebony curls, he was perfection.

When he met her gaze, Kip smiled, pulling her up and pressing her against his heaving chest. "I'm definitely going to need a new desk now," he murmured as he pressed a kiss to her shoulders. "I'll never be able to get any work done."

A knock sounded at the door. "Come on you two. It's starting in five minutes. Let's go."

THREE

KIPLING SQUEEZED Elba's hand as they watched the laptop's glowing screen in silence. The feed showed a small room with just one metal chair in its centre. No table. No windows. Elba took a deep breath, realising she'd been expecting something that looked more like a police interrogation room. This wasn't the police, though. The Men of Magic made their own rules.

Tension rippled from Hemingway in waves as he flexed his fingers against the desk, his dark blue eyes narrowed and his jaw set. Elba considered saying something, but before she could string together the words to try and make him feel better, there was movement on the screen.

Selena, dressed in a dark grey jumpsuit, was thrown into the chair, causing it to screech against the rough, concrete floor. Her hands were bound behind her back and Elba swallowed a gasp at the sight of her. She looked awful. Bruises were blooming on her beautiful face, her plump bottom lip split and swollen. Her luscious brown hair hung limp around her shoulders, which despite her injuries were thrown back in defiance, her dark eyes glittering with rage.

"Who the fuck has done that to her?" Kip hissed.

Hem shook his head, his teeth clenched. "Could be anyone. My money's on Sage."

Kip grunted in agreement and Elba looked between them in confusion. "Who's Sage? Why would they do that to her?"

"Sage's partner was killed last week when we checked on that cluster," Kip explained, his eyes fixed on the screen. "Even though Selena wasn't there, she's still a freedom."

Elba baulked at the ice-cold hatred in his voice. Remembering his sliced body at the hands of Naomi, however, she couldn't really blame him. The Freedoms were cruel and ruthless, hurting anyone who got in their way.

A movement on the screen pulled her attention back to the laptop and she watched as two Men of Magic—a man and a woman—she didn't recognize stalked in front of Selena.

The man, stocky with dark hair and a neat beard, folded his arms across his chest as he stood before her. "Who is the leader of the Freedoms?"

Selena let out a low laugh. "What? Just going right for it? You're not going to buy me a drink first?"

The woman swung an arm forward and back handed Selena across her face, the blow almost knocking her from the chair.

Elba gasped, her eyes wide. The woman's back was to the camera, so she couldn't see her face, just a long brown braid down her spine. Selena lifted her head, spitting blood on the floor at her interrogator's feet.

"I knew you never liked me, Rebecca." She chuckled darkly, spitting another globule of blood on the ground. "How long have you been itching to do that?"

"She knows them?" Elba whispered, as though they might hear her.

Kip have a small nod. "Selena worked here for almost three years. She knows most of the Men."

"What about you, Brent?" Selena continued, tossing her hair from her face. "Do you want to take a swing?"

"Just tell us," Brent said, ignoring her comment. "Who is in charge of the Freedoms? If you tell us, maybe we can come to some sort of deal."

"Surely, we should come up with the deal before I tell you," Selena said, flashing him a bloodstained smile. "Look. I'll tell you what you want to know, on one condition."

Brent unfolded his arms, placing his hands in his pockets as he rolled back on his heels. "Go on. What do you want?"

Selena leaned forward, lowering her voice. "I want you, to suck my dick."

The words had barely left her lips before Brent kicked her chair, sending her toppling backwards, her head smacking into the concrete floor. Elba flinched, her hands flying to her mouth as she yelped.

Hem slammed his hand down on the desk, turning away from the laptop with a growl. "She's trying to get herself killed."

"What?" Elba stared up at him as he dragged his hands through his hair, pulling strands free from the small blond bun in the process.

"She's not going to tell them anything," Kip explained as Hem strode to the window, his hands gripping the narrow frame. "She's hoping if she winds them up enough, they'll kill her and save her the trouble of trying to hold out."

Elba stared. "Would the bureau let that happen? Would they really kill her?"

Kip shrugged, frowning at the screen. "Hopefully someone watching will step in, but it might be too late. I mean, they haven't even started using magic yet."

"That's why she's doing it." Hem groaned, his head resting against the glass. "She knows how much worse it will get if they start using magic."

Elba opened her mouth to ask what he meant, but a strangled cry from the laptop stole the question from her lips. Red sparks streamed from Rebecca's fingers, pulling Selena and her chair back upright, twisting around her.

"Where are the Freedoms?" Rebecca asked, pulling the sparking red magic tighter.

Selena let out a gasp as the magic squeezed the air from her lungs, but she stared down the two Men before her, her eyes blazing with defiance.

"No one's going to save you," Brent said, walking a slow circle around her chair. He paused, kicking at a small dark patch on the floor behind her. She must have split her head open when she fell. "Naomi's dead."

Selena snarled. "I know."

Of course, she did. She might have been frozen in the warehouse during Hemingway's fight with her partner, but she would have been aware of everything. Elba's stomach tightened as she thought of Selena watching Naomi slit her own throat rather than being taken by the bureau; unable to save her.

"Just tell us where the Freedoms are hiding and," Brent jerked his head in Rebecca's direction, "I'll call her off."

"You're all so fucking blind," Selena rasped as the red sparked ropes of magic tightened, draining the colour from her face.

Rebecca raised her other hand, sending a plume of power out that choked the end of her sentence from her lips.

"Tell us!" Brent barked.

Elba gripped the table, barely breathing. Kip's office was silent, the three of them watching in horrified silence as the two Men slowly choked Selena to death.

Brent lashed out with the back of his hand sending blood spraying from Selena's mouth. "Tell us or maybe we pay your family in Venezuela a visit."

Selena's nonplussed expression faltered; alarm clear in her dark brown eyes as she stared up at him. She tried to speak but her voice remained strangled by Rebecca's sparks. Brent jerked his chin in his partner's direction and the flaming rope loosened.

Selena leaned forward, choking at the air, her breath coming in painful gasps. "It didn't work on Naomi," she bit out. "Why do you think it would it work on me?"

Rebecca laughed, cold and low. "Naomi's family had a quick death. We'd make yours suffer. Perhaps we'll make you watch."

Elba's stomach turned and she staggered back from the laptop. "The bureau killed Naomi's family?" she whispered.

Before her, Kip and Hem shared a pained look, their mouths in tight lines.

"We didn't know," Kip said, turning to her. He pushed a hand through his dark curls, his fair complexion even paler. "I didn't think that the bureau was capable of doing something like that."

Elba wrapped her arms around herself, her eyes fixed on the screen in horror as Rebecca lashed out on Selena with a punch that send her head snapping backwards. Kip and Hem didn't even flinch, staring frozen at the screen as Rebecca and Brent took turns kicking and punching her. With each blow her body sagged, the life draining from her.

"We have to make it stop," Elba pleaded. "We can't let them do this."

Hem's expression darkened, his fists clenching as tight as his jaw as he watched the screen. "We're only doing what she did when Naomi sliced Kip up."

Elba baulked, disgust twisting her gut. "That might be true, but what she did wasn't right, and neither is this."

"We couldn't stop it even if we wanted to," Kip said, reaching for her hand. "They can't know we're watching."

Elba stepped out of his reach. "There has to be something we can do. Are you seriously just going to stand by and watch them kill her?"

"They won't kill her," Hem said, his voice so quiet, Elba

turned to look at him. "This is just a taster. They'll take her to stew in her cell and then just as she's got her breath back, they'll give her round two."

Elba stared at the two men beside her. How many times had they been in those rooms? How many people had skirted the edge of death at their hands? Kip seemed to sense the fear —or was it disgust—in her eyes and moved toward her, his face creased with concern.

On the laptop screen, Selena lay on the floor, unmoving, her dark hair covering her face. Rebecca kicked her in the back and Elba flinched, unable to tear her eyes away as Brent bent down and grabbed the neck of her shirt, dragging her from the room, out of sight. Hem reached out and closed the laptop with a soft click.

Elba sank down onto the black leather sofa, trying to keep the bile from rising in her throat. "Will they really torture and kill her family?" she whispered.

A dark cloud passed across Hem's face and he turned to the window, his hands shoved in his pockets.

"You must know her family if you were together that long," Elba pushed. "Even with what Selena did—what she allowed to happen—her family shouldn't have to pay for that. Can we warn them somehow?"

Kipling sat heavily in one of the chairs beside the desk, pulling his hand over his face. "We could try to warn them. Whether they believe us or not is another matter."

"What do you mean?" Elba asked, her arms still wrapped around her middle as though she might be able to comfort herself.

"Her parents aren't Magics," Hem explained. "Her grandfather was, and he managed to help her keep it hidden. He taught her how to control it. He was the one who inspired her to join the Men of Magic. He died a year after she moved to England."

"So, her immediate family have no idea she's magical."

Elba leaned back, helplessness overwhelming her. "We still have to try."

Silence swelled around them until the words Elba had tried to keep inside, burst from her lips. "Do you still think you're the 'good guys'?"

Hem and Kip shared a look, their expressions grim. Her heart panged at the pain she saw there. The bureau was their home—their family. To discover that everything they'd been raised to believe might be nothing more than a lie ... She couldn't imagine what must be going through their heads.

Elba was still trying to think of something to say when a loud knock sounded at the door, causing them all to jump to their feet.

Kipling strode to the door and opened it, Eli and Emilia sweeping in, in a flash of copper and tailored suit.

Eli looked between them, his eyes lingering on Elba as he said, "We need to talk."

FOUR

TENSION FILLED the room as Eli leaned against the large glass desk, folding his arms across his chest as his sister slid into one of the black leather chairs and crossed her legs.

"What happened?" Hem asked, his eyes flitting to the closed laptop on the desk.

Eli followed his gaze and shook his head. "No one knows about the feed. Don't worry."

"If we don't need to worry, tell us what's going on." Kip crossed his arms, his silver eyes like steel.

Emilia flashed him a smile as sharp as a dagger. "We didn't say you didn't need to worry."

"Enough games," Hem growled. "Tell us."

Eli raised his eyebrows before turning his attention to Elba once more. "Perhaps we should have this discussion in private."

Elba opened her mouth to protest, but Kip had already straightened, moving to her side.

"Whatever you need to say, you can say in front of her."

"That serious, huh?" Emilia's auburn eyebrows arched in an identical fashion to her brother.

A low rumbling noise came from Hem's direction, the

impatience and rage rippling from him manifesting in wreaths of black smoke billowing from his hands.

Eli's green eyes sparked as they narrowed. "Calm down, Hemingway. We're here about Selena."

"What about her?" he bit out.

"You know what's going to happen to her, don't you?" Emilia asked, leaning back in the chair and tossing her long copper locks over her shoulder. "What they're going to do."

"Get to the fucking point," Hem ground out.

Elba watched him, eyes wide, as Kip stepped away from her and moved to his friend. His hands lingered at his sides, poised but not touching, as though sensing Hem was about to explode.

"We thought perhaps if you cared enough to risk getting a feed to watch her interrogation," Eli said carefully, eyeing the smoke curling around Hem, "that you might also want to go and say goodbye."

Elba baulked at the word. *Goodbye.* They really were going to kill her. She turned to Kip and Hem, their matching expressions mistrust and pure rage.

"Even if I did," Hem answered slowly, "there's no way I could get down there without clearance, and we know no one is going to give that to me."

Emilia offered that sly, fox-like smile once more. "Which is why we're here. What if we told you we could get you down there without clearance?"

"Why?" Kip asked, his silver eyes narrowed to slits. "Why would you help us?"

Eli chuckled, pressing a hand to his chest. "And here I thought we were friends. Can't friends do nice things for one another?"

"What do you want?" Hem asked.

"Want?" Eli's mouth curled into a smile as he slid his emerald gaze to where Elba stood. "There's a lot of things I want."

Elba shuddered as he slid his eyes over the length of her. Heart thundering, she glanced at Kip to find his fists clenched and his attention fixed on the copper-haired man. The tension in the room was suffocating and it took all her strength to draw in a shaking breath without gasping.

"Stop dicking about," Kip said, his voice laced with ice that Elba hadn't heard before. "What do you want?"

Eli grinned, throwing Elba a wink before crossing an ankle over his knee. "What if we said we would pull in a favour later down the line? We do this for you, and at some point, if we need help, you give it to us. No questions asked."

Elba's eyes widened. Surely Kip and Hem wouldn't agree to this? These two seemed every bit as sly as the foxes their hair colour matched. They might call in something that could get them sacked—or worse. She watched, barely breathing, as a silent conversation passed between the friends.

"Fine," Hem said, his dark blue eyes glacial.

Eli shared a look with his sister, then reached for a notepad and pen, scribbling down what looked like a series of numbers.

"There's an elevator that leads to the floor they have Selena on. It looks like the normal holding cell floor, but it's not. It's further down. This is the code to operate the elevator. Message me when you're ready and I'll make sure the cameras are down for fifteen minutes."

"Fifteen minutes?" Hem scoffed.

Eli tapped the pad against his palm. "You think there aren't people watching the feeds? How long do you think I can make it happen before someone notices? Don't be a greedy bastard. Get down there, say goodbye and get out. Fifteen minutes, or you're on your own."

"Don't even think about trying to link this back to us," Emilia said, getting to her feet and smoothing her skirt. "Everything we've done has been through your log in and IP address."

"Fifteen minutes it is, then," Kip said, holding his hand out for the pad.

Eli held his gaze for a moment before handing it over. Standing, he straightened his jacket, throwing another wink at Elba before moving to the door. "Pleasure as always, gentlemen. Elba."

There was nothing Elba could do but stare as the red-haired twins sauntered from the room. Once the door closed behind them, however, she let out the breath she'd been holding and collapsed on the sofa.

"What the actual fuck was that?" Kip hissed, rounding on Hem. "Are you seriously going to go down there?"

Hem didn't flinch away, squaring his shoulders instead. "No. *We* are going down there."

Elba watched as the two men stared at each other, anger rippling from them in waves. Just as it got too much to bear, Hem sighed.

"Use your bloody head," Hem said, clawing fingers through his hair. "Do you really think I want to go and say goodbye to her?"

Kip lifted his arms at his side. "Why else would you be going? I mean—"

"She did nothing as Naomi almost killed you," Hem interrupted, his voice quiet. "If there was any lingering part of me that still loved her, that snuffed it out."

The fury circling Kipling's broad shoulders dissipated as he dipped his head with a sigh. "Why, then? Why risk it?"

Hem sank down onto the sofa beside Elba, giving her a small, sad smile. "Because maybe we can get her to tell us where the Freedoms are before the bureau kills her."

Elba stared at him, her eyes wide. "You're going to let them kill her?"

"We're limited with what we can do here. I don't like it, but we can't save her." Hem looked away, leaning his head on the back of the sofa and closing his eyes. "If we find the Freedoms, we get answers. I know there are Men who swapped allegiance and I want to hear both sides of the story."

Kip groaned, slumping down in the seat Emilia had been sitting in. "This is so needlessly reckless."

"How else are we going to get answers?" Hem asked. "They put restrictors in us. Our entire lives, they've been lying to us."

Elba's heart contracted at the pain that flashed across Kip's face. "How do you know she'll tell you?"

"She doesn't know we found the restrictors," Kip muttered, his silver eyes shuttered. "If we show her. If we tell her we want to find the truth, she'll help us."

Elba swallowed. "And if she doesn't?"

Hem turned to her, his eyes cold. "What does she have to lose?"

They sat in silence for a minute until Elba could no longer hold in her question. "Why do you think Eli and Emilia offered to help?"

Hem snorted and returned his head, eyes closed, to the back of the sofa.

Kip met her gaze from beneath his dark lashes. "That's the scariest part. This could just be a trap. I don't know what—or who—we can trust anymore."

"I can just imagine us down there, on some storage floor, being ambushed and hauled off." Hem groaned.

Elba drew a trembling breath and straightened her shoulders. "That's why you're going to bring me with you."

Kip sat up straight, his milky skin paling further. "Absolutely not."

It was a fight to control the urge to clench her fingers into fists, but Elba took a deep breath instead. "It's because of me that you're both still here. If Hem hadn't brought me to the warehouse, you'd never have beaten Naomi."

"It's also your fault that we're in this mess in the first place," Hem retorted, but there was no malice in his words.

Elba folded her arms across her chest. "Just because you decided to unleash magic next to a main road, does not make this my fault."

Gentle hands on her legs caused Elba to break the glare she was unleashing on Hemingway, and she turned to find that Kip had slipped from his seat to kneel before her. He reached for her hands, his silver eyes shimmering as he looked up at her.

"What happened in that warehouse," he said, his thumbs stroking the back of her hands, "was a fluke. There's no way we should have left there alive."

"A fluke?" Elba repeated, pulling her hands away.

Kip tightened his grip. "Not like that. You . . . I mean—"

"You were amazing." Hem sighed, shaking his head at his friend. "You learnt three complicated spells, faced Magics ten times more powerful and then took it upon yourself to channel Kip's power through the conduit stone as some sort of human battery pack. You were incredible."

Elba gave him a grateful smile. "Thank you."

"I'm more than aware how amazing Elba is, thank you." Kipling shot Hem a glare. "But do you really think we'll be that lucky twice?"

"We only need luck if Eli and Emilia are planning to turn us in," Hem said with a shrug. "If they're telling the truth and just being the sly, intense weirdos they usually are, then it's fifteen minutes and we're done. No magic required."

Elba watched as Kip dipped his head, resting it briefly on her lap before looking at the two of them, his face pained. "I have a really bad feeling about this."

"I've had a bad feeling since we stepped in this building," Hem replied, his jaw tight.

A terse silence settled over them and Elba looked between the two men, forcing a smile. "Right. Which one of you is making me invisible?"

Kipling looked up at her, his eyes pleading, but Elba stared him down.

"It's fifteen minutes, Kip," Hem said, sitting forward and clapping a hand on his shoulder.

Before Kip could retort, Hem muttered the string of words that sent a shiver across her body as though someone had dropped a sheet over her. It felt different than before, and she wondered whether it was a different spell.

Kip's hands lingered on her leg, his fingers tensed as though scared to let her go. Elba smiled, even though she knew he couldn't see and leaned forward, pressing a kiss to his lips.

"Right, guys," Hem said, staring at his phone. "I've messaged Eli. Let's get going."

FIVE

ELBA FOLLOWED behind as they walked down the long corridor of offices. Hem was staring at his phone, frowning at the set of instructions Eli had sent.

"We'd have seen it before if it was down here," Kip mumbled. "We've worked on this corridor for years."

Hem didn't look up from his phone. Their footsteps were quiet on the thin dark grey carpet, and Elba was thankful that the offices didn't have windows looking onto the corridor, even though the monotony of never-ending doors was making her a little dizzy.

"Here," Hem said, coming to a stop at a supply closet.

Kip snorted. "You can't be serious."

"Maybe we're giving them too much credit. Perhaps they're just plain messing with us."

Elba reached between them and tried the handle, the door swinging open into the corridor.

"Shit a brick, Elba." Hem gasped. "Could you please refrain from pulling that Casper crap?"

Any smile that had started to creep onto Elba's lip faded as she took in the sight beyond the door. An elevator, with only one button for 'down' was concealed inside the cupboard. Ominous didn't begin to describe it.

"Here we go," Kip said, stabbing the button.

Hem looked at his watch. "Fifteen minutes and counting."

When the doors slid open, they paused before stepping inside. There were no mirrors and no buttons, just a small keypad. Elba swallowed as she watched the look Kip gave Hem before he pulled the piece of paper from his pocket and typed out the code.

As the box dropped like a stone, Elba slid her hand into Kipling's. He squeezed, his eyes fixed ahead, and she noted sparks of magic flickering from the both of them—ready for whatever lay on the other side of the doors. The descent seemed to go on forever. Surely nothing could be this far down? Glancing up at the clenched jaws on either side of her, she tried to calm her pounding heart.

Without a display showing the floors, the slowing and stopping of the elevator caught her off guard and she stumbled as the doors slid apart. Hem pressed his hand against the frame, keeping them open, while he peered out, checking. In front of them, stretched a long dark corridor lined with glass windows that seemed to glow with a pale blue light.

"What is this place?" Elba whispered.

Kipling frowned, taking a small step out of the elevator. "It's the same as the holding floor, but—"

"Wrong," Hem finished with a shudder.

They stepped out into the corridor and the doors hissed shut behind them.

"Nine minutes," Kip muttered, glancing at his watch.

Elba's heart sped up. How would they possibly have enough time to do what they needed to do?

Hem was already striding down the corridor, peering through the windows, looking for Selena. After just four however, he slowed to a halt. As Elba hurried to catch up, she realised why.

Behind each window was a prisoner. She'd been expecting prisoners, but not like this. Her hand moved to her mouth, her eyes wide as she took in the emaciated, beaten and bloodied figures bound and cowering in the corners.

"Who are they?" Elba whispered.

Kip was shaking beside her. She looked up to see flames dancing in his eyes and realised it was with rage. "Freedoms."

"I recognise this one," Hem said, staring through the window. "We brought him in a couple of weeks ago."

"What did you think happened to them after you brought them in?" Elba asked.

Hem turned to her, his face pale as his eyes flickered over the empty space where she stood. "I didn't think. I . . ."

His words trailed off into the darkness and Kip squeezed his shoulder.

"Come on. Let's find Selena. We're running out of time."

Selena was in a cell about halfway down the row. Whether she sensed their presence or not, she didn't look up. Curled in a corner, blood was smeared across the smooth metal walls and coated her grey sweats.

Hem knocked on the glass. "Selena?"

She stiffened before turning to face us, each movement clearly causing agony. Elba wondered just how many bones broken during her interrogation had been left untreated.

"What the hell are you doing here?" She spat.

Hem frowned, but Elba could see the concern in his dark blue eyes—the tenseness of his body—as he took in her broken form.

"Look. We only have a few minutes," he said. "I'll warn your family. I'll try to keep them safe."

Selena's dark eyes widened, relief flooding her features. "Really?"

"Yes." He glanced down the corridor as if to check no one had appeared. "Tell us where the Freedoms are."

Her face crumpled with rage. "I knew it!" she hissed. "They sent you down here, didn't they?"

"No, they didn't," Kip said. "We listened to what Naomi said. We found the restrictors."

Doubt flickered across her face as she looked between the two of them. "I don't believe you."

Hem held up a hand and a column of thick, glittering smoke encompassed his fingers, pouring up toward the ceiling. Beside him, Kip did the same, summoning a ball of white flame bright enough to shame the sun. Elba stepped back, shielding her eyes.

Once the smoke and flames had vanished, she blinked and found Selena smiling, her white teeth stained pink with blood.

"Feels good, right?"

Kip glanced at his watch again. "Selena, we have four minutes to get back in that elevator before the security cameras come back on. Tell us where the Freedoms are."

She shook her head. "I can't."

"No." Hem ground out. "You won't."

"What do I have to gain?" she asked. "They're going to kill me soon. Unless you're threatening me? I tell you or you don't warn my family?"

Hem growled. "You know I'd warn your family either way. I'm not the monster here."

Darkness flashed in Selena's eyes. "Who *is* the monster?"

"That's what we're trying to figure out," Kip pleaded. "Tell us so we can get answers. Please."

Selena slumped her head back against the wall and closed her eyes. For a moment, Elba thought they were finished. Then, she opened her eyes, sliding her gaze towards them.

"The Dog and Gun. Ask for Lawrence."

"Thank you," Kip said, already moving away from the glass back towards the elevator. "Are you there El?"

Elba brushed her hand against his as she tried to keep up

with his stride. It took her a moment to realise that Hem was still standing, staring at the glass.

"Hem!" she hissed. "Come on!"

He raised his hand to place it on the glass, but dropped it at the last second, giving Selena a sort of nod instead as he turned and sprinted towards the elevator.

Kip had already pressed the button, but the doors weren't opening. Elba's heart thudded in her throat as she stared at the metal doors. What if it arrived and people were in there? She was about to whisper her concerns when they opened, and she almost sank to the floor with relief to see it empty.

No one spoke as the elevator sped upwards and silence prevailed as they hurried back along the corridor. Elba blinked as they continued past Kip's office. She looked up at the two men as they strode, stone faced, ahead of her and understood. What they'd seen down there—the creeping doubt of what the bureau really was—was starting to deepen. It wasn't safe to talk about it here. Not even a word.

Hem muttered under his breath as they reached the main elevator at the other end of the corridor and Elba felt herself shimmer back into existence. They travelled down to the lobby in the same tense silence and Elba shuddered as she thought of how different things had been when they travelled up to Kip's office just an hour or two earlier.

As they stalked across the lobby, eyes forward, Elba tried not to break into a run as desperation to get out of the building choked her lungs. Hem held out a palm, pushing the glass doors open, in too much of a hurry to deal with the revolving door at the centre of the entrance. Kip reached out, grabbing hold of her wrist and tugged her down the side of the building after Hem. Elba didn't have a chance to ask what was going on before she was swallowed by silver flames.

SIX

THE GROUND SOLIDIFIED under Elba's feet in Hemingway's apartment.

"Fuck!" Hem shouted, his fingers fisting his hair. "What the fuck was that? Fuck."

Elba looked to Kip, expecting him to try and calm Hemingway down, but instead she found him sinking onto the sofa, his eyes distant. Panic fluttered in her chest as she watched their world crumble. Everything they'd ever known called into question—tainted.

"You really had no idea?" she asked.

Hem wheeled on her. "Of course not! Do you really think we'd be okay with a fucking . . ." he thrust his hands in the air searching for the word, "*dungeon* beneath us?"

Elba raised her eyebrows. "You've killed Freedoms before. You've tortured them—"

"Interrogated," Hem interrupted.

Elba snorted. "Really? I've seen how the Men of Magic 'interrogate' people."

"That's different," Hem said, his eyes wide in desperation.

As much as Elba's heart ached to see these two men who she cared so much about hurting, she found herself shaking her head. "Really? Is it? Just because it involves someone you know this time? You said that a lot of Freedoms used to be Men. I bet if you looked closer in those cells, you'd see more people you knew."

Hem gaped at her, the hurt glistening in his eyes like an open wound. Elba clenched her hands into fists at her side. She wouldn't apologise for the truth. They needed to hear it. They'd been so wrapped up in the bureau—their saviours—for so long, they may as well have been brainwashed.

"I don't understand," Kip murmured from the couch, his head in his hands. "How do they get away with it?"

Frustration bubbled and fizzed in Elba's gut. "Magic," she ground out. "Are you both really this blind? Have you really no idea what it's like for Normals? For most people on the planet?"

Kip gave a small groan and Elba swallowed, knowing she should probably take her foot off the gas a little, but she needed them to wake up—to stop sulking—and fight.

"The Freedoms want to upset the balance, though," Hem insisted, although the fight behind the words was fading. "They want to wipe out the Normals."

Elba sighed. "Do they?"

"This is why we need to go and meet this Lawrence, whoever he is." Kip ran his hands through his dark curls and tipped his head back, staring at the ceiling.

"Honestly," Elba said, watching as Hem sank down onto an armchair, his tanned face pale. "What did you think the bureau was doing to the Freedoms you captured?"

Hem shared a look with Kip before turning to her. "Blockers. There's a way to block someone's magic—make them Normal. If you did that and erased their memory . . ."

"They'd have no idea they had magic," Elba breathed, her eyes wide. "That's awful."

Kip barked a sour laugh. "More awful than being kept, chained and beaten in a dark cell?"

Elba stared at the two broken men before her, her heart aching. She walked to Hem and took hold of his hand, hoisting him up from his seat and leading him over to the sofa. Sitting down beside Kip she patted the seat next to her and as he slumped down, and she wrapped her arms around them both.

"It's going to be okay," she soothed. "We'll get answers and then you can decide what to do."

Hem huffed a sigh on her shoulder, his warm breath tickling her collarbone. "What *can* we do, though?"

"It's not like we can go up against the GW," Kip said, lacing his fingers with hers and bringing them to his lips.

"That's just it," Hem said. "I don't understand how the GW is allowing this to happen."

Elba frowned, looking between the tops of their heads resting on her shoulders. "GW? Like the car?"

Kip sat up a little, laughter dancing in his silver eyes. "No. The Grand Wizard."

Laughter burst from Elba's lips. "The *what*?"

A smile pulled at Kipling's lips. "It's an old term. Older than history itself."

"The Grand Wizard?" Elba tried to bite back the laughter rising in her throat once more. "Go on, then. Who is he?"

Hem sat up, ducking out from under her arm but giving her hand a squeeze of thanks before shifting to face her. "The Grand Wizard is the highest of the high. His magic outweighs everyone else's and is the conduit through which all our magic flows. It's like a failsafe. If something happens to him, all magic dies. He's got security like you wouldn't believe."

Elba blinked. "All magic? Like everyone in the country?"

Kip chuckled softly, his nose nuzzling her neck. "Everyone in the world."

"Have you ever seen him?" she asked, trying and failing to imagine someone that powerful.

Hem shook his head. "No. No one really does. His identity is kept under lock and key."

"What happens when he dies?" Elba asked.

"It passes down through the blood line," Kip said. "If I remember correctly, he has a daughter who it would go to next."

Elba frowned. "Could someone intercept that?"

"What? Like steal the magic?" Hem shifted, untying and retying his hair.

"I suppose there might be a way to do it, but to even get close to him . . ." Kip frowned.

"Could that be what the Freedoms want?" she asked. "To get to the Grand Wizard?"

Hem cringed. "You've got to stop calling him that."

"Sorry, but I'm not calling him the GW, like he's some sort of nineties rapper."

"Fine." Hem rolled his eyes playfully. "I guess that's just one of the many things we'll find out if Selena actually gave us a lead."

"Do you think she'd lie to us?" Elba asked.

Hem's eyes shuttered and he turned to lean back against the sofa. "I honestly don't know."

"What's next, then?" Elba asked. "Do we go and find that place? With a name like 'Dog and Gun', I'm assuming it's a pub."

"Tomorrow," Kip said, his face grim. "Hem needs to contact Selena's family. It'll probably take a while."

Elba watched as Hem paled further, pushing himself off the couch and traipsing into the kitchen. He pulled a bottle of wine from the rack and grabbed a glass from the side.

"You want one?" he asked, not even turning to them as he poured a very large glass of red.

Elba looked at Kipling, finding him watching his friend with a look of grave concern on his beautiful face. "I think I'm going to go home."

Kip turned to her then, something flickering in his silver eyes. "You don't have to go."

"You two need some time to process," she said, before leaning in to Kip. "And he needs you."

Kip's mouth pressed into a tight line, his eyes still fixed on Hem as he took large swigs from his glass. "Okay. Let me take you."

Elba placed her hand on his arm, giving it a gentle squeeze. "No. I'll call a taxi. It's fine. He needs you. You need each other."

Kip exhaled, tearing his eyes away from the picture of despair in the kitchen. "Let me walk you out at least."

"I'll see you tomorrow, Hem," Elba called as she pulled out her phone on the way to the door. "Don't even think about going to the Dog and Gun without me."

Hemingway mumbled something and raised his glass in a half salute. Elba's stomach clenched. It was painful seeing him so lacklustre. It was as though someone had turned down a dimmer switch, muting his warm, golden energy.

"He'll be okay," Kip whispered as he unlocked and opened the door.

Elba nodded, but as he pulled the door closed behind them, she placed a hand on his chest and looked up at him. "Will *you* be okay?"

Kip smiled and cupped her face in his hands, pressing a kiss to her lips. "I'll be fine. It's just a lot to process."

Her phone vibrated and she glanced down at the notification. "Taxi will be here in three minutes."

"Are you sure you don't want me to take you?"

Elba rose up on her tiptoes and pressed a kiss to his lips. "Hem needs you more than me tonight."

Kip frowned, his mouth opening to speak, but at the last minute he pulled her forward into a kiss instead. Elba slid her hands around his waist, savouring the warmth of his body through his shirt. Kip held her tight against his chest and she sighed, opening up to him as he stroked her tongue with his. A small moan escaped her lips and he answered with one of his own, turning and pressing her to the wall. Elba's hands stroked up his back, twisting in his hair as he pushed his hard body against hers.

A car honked its horn outside and she pulled back, breathless.

"I'll see you in the morning," she said, stroking her palms down the hard planes of his chest.

Kip's frown had returned, his mouth a tight line.

"What's wrong?" she asked. "Is it the bureau? Selena?"

His expression softened and he shook his head. "I . . . I'll miss you."

Elba grinned as his cheeks pinkened and he looked away. "Aww. Was that really so hard to say?" She reached up and cupped his face, rising to kiss him once again, her heart swelling at the perfect softness of his lips. "I'll miss you, too."

A small smile kicked at the corner of his mouth as he took her hands in his and squeezed. "I'll come get you tomorrow morning."

She smiled back and let his fingers fall from hers. "I look forward to it."

Elba was still fuzzy with warmth as she leaned her head against the window of the taxi, her heart twice its normal size. Whatever it was between them was so much more intense than anything she'd ever felt before. Maybe it was the magic. Maybe it was the life and death nature of what had happened between them. Elba smiled, thinking of how nervous Kip had been telling her that he would miss her. It was nice seeing his vulnerable side—the side she'd first seen at the Italian restaurant.

A sharp ache bit at her chest. Kipling had been given up by his family as a child because of his magic, placing all his love and trust in the bureau. Hemingway too. Elba could only imagine the angst and heartache the two men must be trying to process right now. Even without finding out the truth, it was pretty clear the bureau was not the shining example of righteousness they'd portrayed themselves to be.

Lost in her own thoughts, Elba barely registered paying for the taxi and wandering into her building. It was only when she reached the top of the stairs to find her door closed but unlocked that she halted, her heartrate skyrocketing.

Selena was locked up. Naomi was dead. Could more Freedoms have found her? She didn't know where the conduit stone was. Kipling had put it somewhere and she hadn't asked. Barely breathing, Elba slid her phone into her hand and unlocked it, ready to call for help. It was then, that she heard it. Someone was singing inside her apartment.

Elba's fingers gripped her phone, anger rippling in her gut as her teeth clenched. She wrenched open the door and strode through the door. "What the fuck are you doing here, Alex?"

The singing stopped abruptly.

Standing in her kitchen, stirring something in a saucepan, stood her ex-boyfriend, tanned and half naked, acting like the last three months hadn't happened.

"Elba! Hey." He turned around, the grin plastered on his face faltering as he took in her incredulous expression.

"What. The. Fuck. Are. You. Doing. Here?"

The smile melted from his lips. "I came home."

Blood roared in Elba's ears. "This is not your home. It stopped being your home when you pissed off to Thailand without so much as a goodbye. It stopped being your home when you cleared out our savings to go and fuck around on a beach somewhere."

Hurt flashed in his brown eyes, but she couldn't bring herself to care. He needed to get the hell out of her apartment. He looked different to the last time she'd seen him. He was leaner and deeply tanned, his light brown hair longer and shaggier, giving him an unkempt backpacker look. She supposed that's what he was.

"I haven't got anywhere else to go," he said, leaning against the counter.

Elba folded her arms across her chest. "I don't give two shits. Go to your mum's place."

"Elba—"

"Don't 'Elba' me," she snapped. "Get out. And give me your key while you're at it."

Alex shoved a hand through his mop of hair and sighed. "Seriously. You need to chill out."

"Chill out?" she repeated. "I've just come home to find someone in my apartment. You're lucky I haven't called the police."

"I used to live here. My name's on the lease." Alex frowned, folding his own arms.

Elba scowled. "No, it's not. I had it removed when I renewed last month. So, right now, you're trespassing."

"Fine," he bit out. "Can I at least stay here tonight? It'll take me four hours by train to get to Mum's. I'll book a ticket for first thing in the morning."

Elba stared at him, her arms still folded and her heart slamming against her chest.

"Please, El?" he pleaded. "I'll sleep on the couch."

Elba snorted. "I'd think so! There's no chance you're getting near my bed."

A small smile tugged at his lips. "Does that mean you're letting me stay?"

Elba threw her keys in the bowl and slammed the door shut. "You leave first thing in the morning. I don't want to talk to you. I don't want to see you. Stay the fuck out of my way."

Before he could respond, she strode past him into her bedroom, slamming the door behind her. Her head was spinning and her stomach churning. Alex was back. He was in her apartment. She gulped at the air.

Throwing herself down onto the bed, she tried to calm her

42

screaming heart. The familiar smell of sea salt and citrus flooded her senses, her bedcovers laced with Kipling's scent. She inhaled deep, her chest tightening at the thought of what had happened between those sheets over the last twenty-four hours.

Alex's singing crept in under the closed door and she groaned, burying her head in the pillow. One night. That was all it was. She could ignore him for one night and then he'd be out of her life forever.

Elba stifled a yawn. She'd barely slept over the past couple of days and exhaustion tore at her. Before she could consider whether it was a good idea, sleep took the choice from her hands.

SEVEN

IT WAS ONLY as Elba stumbled, bleary eyed, into the kitchen the next morning that she remembered.

"Good morning!"

She palmed her face with a groan. Had Alex always been this cheerful? It was beyond irritating. His clothes were scattered around the living room, draped over the back of the couch. His suitcase was overspilling on the floor by the bathroom.

She turned to him, cooking bacon—her bacon—on the stove, in nothing but his underwear. "Make yourself at home, why don't you?"

Alex turned and grinned at her. "I forgot how grumpy you are in the morning. I've boiled the kettle. Let me make you a coffee."

"Put some damn clothes on."

He chuckled. "It's nothing you haven't seen before."

Elba sank down onto a chair. "That's not the point. You do realise we broke up, right?"

"You've made that very clear," he said as he scooped coffee into a mug. She couldn't help but notice it was her favourite one.

"No," she said. "*You* made that clear when you fucked off to Thailand."

He turned around and handed her the mug. "If you want me to apologise, I'm not going to."

She snorted. "I wouldn't expect you to. You're a selfish prick."

He exhaled and returned to the stove, leaving Elba to inhale the soothing aroma of the coffee.

"I've booked my train."

Elba looked up from her mug. "What time?"

"Eleven," he replied. "I'll be out of your hair soon enough."

Relief flooded through her. "Don't forget to leave your key."

She saw his shoulders tense at her tone, but it only made her want to sink the knife in deeper.

He opened a cupboard and pulled out a loaf of bread. "Will you not be here to say goodbye?"

Elba watched him, irked at the ease he moved around her kitchen. Not only remembering where everything was but helping himself. "No," she said. "I have plans."

"Are you still working at the same place?"

She gripped her mug tighter. After what had happened at the warehouse with Kip, she'd called in sick, claiming the flu. If she took any more time off, she was going to need a doctor's note, or she'd lose her job. Saba had messaged a few times, and she'd managed to keep her at bay. The lie wouldn't hold for much longer.

Elba's stomach churned. The idea of going back to the dreary monotony of the office while Kipling and Hemingway dealt with the magical underworld was unbearable. But she wasn't a Magic, so what else could she do?

"Elba?"

She looked up to find Alex holding out a plate with a bacon sandwich on it, his eyebrows raised.

"You zoned out," he said, placing the plate on the table. "Are you at work today? Same place?"

"No. I mean, I'm at the same place, but I'm not working. I've got some time off."

He watched her as though he was going to say something else, but then he took his own plate and sat down at the table instead. Elba squirmed in her seat. She needed to get out of there. Glancing at the clock, she realised she hadn't set a time for Kipling to pick her up. Her phone was in the bedroom, she needed to message and warn him not to magic into the apartment. He'd have to wipe Alex's memory.

"Thanks for breakfast," Elba said, pushing back her chair. "I'm going to eat as I get ready."

Hurt flashed in Alex's eyes, but all it did was make her want to empty the rest of her coffee in his lap. He stood as well, and she winced at his underpants, covered with tiny robots. She remembered them. He'd always worn his underwear until it literally fell apart.

"Look, I know you hate me, but we had some good times before it all got fucked, didn't we?" he asked.

Elba exhaled. "I guess."

"After today, you never have to see me again. It's one of the reasons I came here before going to Mum's. I wanted to say goodbye properly."

She frowned, moving to pick up her plate and mug. "Goodbye."

"Elba." He stepped towards her, his eyes pleading. "I'm not sorry I went, but I am sorry I hurt you. I honestly didn't mean to cause you so much pain."

A thousand razor sharp retorts formed on her tongue, but as she met his gaze and saw the pain and regret there, she was struck by utter exhaustion. She was tired. So tired of holding on to the anger and hate. It was time to let it go.

"Fine," she said, her shoulders slumping. "I'm not sure what you want me to say."

He gave her a small smile and reached for her hand, squeezing it in his. "I don't want you to say anything."

Elba shrugged and moved to pull her hand back, but he held tight.

"If you're not going to be here when I leave, can we at least have a goodbye hug?" he asked. "I need to know that you don't hate me."

Anger flared in her gut. Of course, this was all about him and how he was feeling. A large part of her wanted to refuse to ease his guilt, but that tiredness weighed heavy on her heart.

"Whatever," she muttered, allowing him to pull her to him.

Elba cringed at the feel of his naked chest against her, the once familiar feel of his arms so wrong in a million different ways. She moved to pull away, but he wrapped his arms tighter around her.

"Alex?" she mumbled against his chest. "That's enough."

She was about to knee him in the balls, when silent flames swelled and flickered on the other side of the room. Kip materialised for only a few seconds, the smile on his handsome face fading as fast as the flames surrounding him as he took in the sight of Elba in Alex's arms.

She opened her mouth to call to him, but the flames swallowed him, and he was gone.

"What was that?" Alex asked, looking over his shoulder. "I could have sworn the TV came on for a second."

Elba shoved hard against his chest and ran to her bedroom. Swiping up her phone with trembling hands she swiped through her contacts until she came to Kip's number. She paced her room as it rang and rang. After three tries she threw the phone down on the bed, staring at it as she fisted her hands in her hair. She didn't have Hemingway's number.

She could only imagine what it must have looked like to him. Alex's clothes strewn everywhere and him in only his underwear. It was no matter that she was fully dressed, still wearing her clothes from the night before. He probably hadn't even noticed.

Elba closed her eyes, replaying the hurt and disbelief that had spread across his face before he disappeared. She needed to get to his apartment before they left.

It was only after she'd changed into jeans and a long-sleeved t-shirt, that she realised. She knew roughly where their building was, but she didn't know the exact location or even the floor they were on. They'd always magicked to and from Hemingway's apartment.

Her heart was in her stomach as she marched across to the bathroom, ignoring Alex's questions as he trailed behind her. She slammed the bathroom door shut and locked it. There was only one other thing she could do. She'd have to meet them at the Dog and Gun. While she brushed her teeth, she searched on her phone. There were two pubs with that name, but one was miles away. She hoped against hope it was the one in the centre of the city. If it wasn't there was no way she'd have time to go to the other one.

Quickly typing out a message asking him to call her, she unlocked the bathroom door and started gathering her things.

"Elba?" Alex asked, still hanging around in his under-wear. "What's wrong?"

She paused in the pulling on of her ankle boots to glare at him. "You have fucked up my life for the last time," she ground out. "Get your shit packed up and leave. If you're still here when I get back, I'm calling the police."

Before he could respond, she grabbed her keys and opened the front door.

"Elba—"

"Don't forget to leave your damn key," she called over her shoulder.

An hour. She could be at the pub in an hour if there were

no delays on the underground. She just hoped it would be in time.

EIGHT

ELBA HAD ORDERED a coffee but still hadn't touched it. It sat, stone cold before her, a thin murky film over the top. It was only eleven in the morning and the barman had looked at her in surprise when she'd walked in, having only just unlocked the doors. She wondered if he knew she'd already been waiting outside for half an hour.

It was a nice little place. Tucked down a narrow alleyway, it wasn't the 'old man's pub' the name portrayed it to be. It was somewhere between gastro pub and wine bar, small enough to be a hidden gem that was only found by word of mouth. Elba supposed that was the point. At this time on a Sunday, the only other people inside were the barman and the elderly gentleman who had been nursing a pint for the last twenty-five minutes.

She felt sick. Tracing her finger along the edge of the polished, dark wood table, Elba sucked in small breaths. What if this was the wrong pub? What if it was the right one and when they arrived, Kip wouldn't talk to her?

He'd have to. She'd make sure of it.

In the hour she'd been waiting, anger had flickered in her gut once or twice. Anger that he didn't trust her—that he didn't know she would never do that to him. Elba inhaled a steady breath through her nose. He had no reason to trust her. Trust was earned, and she'd known him less than a fortnight. As much as she already couldn't imagine her life without him, the hard truth was he didn't know her, and she didn't know him. The thought carved a chasm through her chest. Not only at the bitter realisation, but that now she might never get the chance.

When the door finally opened, her stomach rolled. She balled her hands into fists, hardly daring to breath, but it wasn't them. Instead, a scrawny teenage boy strolled up and handed a bundle of newspapers to the barman before sauntering back out again. Elba exhaled, the beginnings of tears burning her eyes. Her phone sat on the table, the screen dark. He hadn't read her messages. Perhaps he'd blocked her. That glimmer of anger rippled again. Would he really not give her the chance to explain?

Elba was so lost in her spiralling emotions that she didn't register the teenager muttering as he stepped back to let someone past. It took her a few moments to realise who had strode into the pub. Her breath stuck in her throat as she watched them. Hem was wearing a khaki green utility jacket and worn jeans. Kip wore smart, dark jeans, a thin dark blue sweater and a worn leather jacket. It was strange to see them without the suits she'd become so accustomed to. It was even stranger to watch them, unaware they were being watched. They were breathtakingly gorgeous.

Elba sat, frozen, unsure what to do—what to say. It was only for a moment, however, before Hem scanned the bar. His dark blue eyes landed on her, widening in surprise before softening as he reached out and placed a hand on Kip's arm.

Elba couldn't move, her heart weighing her down. She watched as Kip turned, the frown lining his beautiful face slipping as he finally noticed her. All she could do was stare. She wanted to get up—to walk to him—but her legs had stopped working. What if he turned away and ignored her? What would she do?

Hem leaned into him, whispering something in his ear, before turning to the barman. Kip stood staring at her for a moment more—his face unreadable—before starting towards her.

"Why are you here?" he asked as he came to a stop by her table.

The harshness of the words drew a sharp breath from her. "Why do you think I'm here?"

He shook his head, glancing over his shoulder at where Hemingway stood talking to the barman. "You should go."

Elba dug her nails into her palm in an attempt to stem the tears forming in her eyes. "Kip . . ."

"It's fine." He sighed and ran a hand through his dark curls. "We didn't say we were exclusive or anything."

Elba watched, eyes wide, as though he was slipping away between her fingers and she was powerless to stop it. He had been going to put her as his contact at the bureau. He'd got her a linking ring . . .

The ring.

She lifted her hand and touched a finger to the thin, simple silver band. Just two days ago, he'd read her feelings through the ring and told her he felt the same.

Glancing up at him, Elba found him staring at the ring. She wondered whether he was remembering, too.

"What can you feel?" she whispered.

Kip's fingers moved to his own ring, pain flickering across his face. Was it her pain or his own he was feeling?

"You said, no more running." Elba swallowed, drawing a shaky breath. If she was going to lose him, it wasn't going to be without a fight. "This feels a lot like running."

His jaw clenched, his lips pressing together.

"Sit," she said. "Please?"

He pulled out one of the wooden chairs and sat, his eyes darting to Hem. "Who is he?"

Elba blew out a slow breath, considering her words as Kip looked ready to flee at any second. "That was Alex."

"Tosser ex-boyfriend, Alex?" he said, eyebrows raised.

She nodded. "He was in my apartment when I got back. I told him to get out, but he fed me some sob story about his mum's house being far away and agreed to get the first available train in the morning if I let him sleep on the sofa."

Kip stared at the table with such intensity, Elba wondered if it would burst into flame. When he didn't speak, she continued.

"I was too tired to argue with him. When I got up this morning, he was parading around in his underwear acting like he lived there. I almost poured my coffee over him."

Kip's frown deepened, his gaze still fixed on the table. "Was that before or after what I saw?"

"I told him I wasn't going to be there when he left and to have a nice life. He acted all hurt and said he needed a hug to know that I didn't hate him." She shuddered. "That's what you saw. I do hate him, though. He already fucked up my life once and now he's done it again." Her voice cracked and she bit down on her lip.

Kip's fingers slid around hers, unfurling her fist. His thumbs brushed against the deep, red crescents her nails had imprinted on her palms. Elba watched his long, pale fingers—too scared to move her own or look up, in fear of what she might see on his face.

"Everything's falling apart," he said, his voice quiet. "Everything I thought I knew is being flipped on its head, and I don't know which way is up. You've been like a lighthouse in the storm, Elba. Something I could head for, somewhere safe. When I magicked in and saw you in another man's arms, I just . . ."

Elba placed her hand over the top of his, her chest aching. "I would never."

He gave the smallest of nods. "I overreacted. I'm sorry."

"I understand." She took a breath, her entire body tense. She wanted to ask whether they were okay—where they stood now—but she couldn't bring herself to form the words.

Kip squeezed her hand and pulled away. "Maybe we should cool things off a little. My head's a mess and I don't want . . ." He palmed a hand across his face. "I don't want to hurt you."

She dropped her gaze to the table as nausea swept through her. Couldn't he tell, that's exactly what he was doing?

"Have you two kids sorted yourselves out yet?"

Elba looked up to find Hemingway standing at the table, a wary smile on his face. It faltered as he took in her expression and he turned to his friend. "You okay?"

Kip nodded, a weak smile curving his lips. "Yeah. I over-reacted like a prick."

"No surprise there then," Hem replied. His eyes flitted between them, still unsure. "I asked the barman about Lawrence."

Elba's eyes widened. "And?"

"And, he said that if people want to speak to Lawrence, they have to send a message. If he deigns to speak to the person, he'll come here."

Kip frowned as Hem turned a chair around and sat down, bracing his arms along the wooden slatted back. "Did you send a message?"

"Of course, I did." He peered into Elba's coffee cup and wrinkled his nose. "I told him that we were Men who had found and removed their restrictors. I also said Selena told us to speak to him."

"How did you send the message?" Elba asked.

Hem chuckled. "Please tell me you're not picturing owls or some shit like that?"

Elba blushed. "No. Of course not."

"I wrote it down on a piece of paper," Hem said, shaking his head. "Whether the paper itself goes to Lawrence or the barman texts it to him, I have no idea."

Kip leaned back, folding his arms. "Do we have a time frame?"

"Nope." Hem shrugged. "But we have no other plans, so I guess we make ourselves comfortable."

Kip sighed before turning to Elba. "You should go. It could be dangerous."

"Absolutely not," she scoffed. "I'm here and I'm staying."

Kip stared at her. "We can't make you invisible and you have no powers. It's not safe."

"Give me powers, then," she said, returning his stare. She was seeing this through whether he liked it or not.

"I could go to the toilet and fetch the conduit stone," Hem offered, looking between them. "It's not a problem."

Elba broke the stare and turned to him. "The conduit stone is in the toilet?"

"No." Hem smirked. "But I can't magic away in the middle of the pub, can I?"

She felt her face redden again. "Oh. That makes sense."

"Shall I then?" Hem asked, trying to catch Kip's eye.

He shrugged. "Whatever. If she wants to continually put herself in danger, it's up to her."

Hem stared at him for a moment more, before standing from the chair and marching off in the direction of the toilets, muttering under his breath.

The tension between them was too much to bear, so Elba stood. "I'm going to get another coffee. Do you want anything?"

Kip stared up at her, his silver eyes unreadable. "Sure. Americano, please."

She nodded and headed to the bar. For almost ten glorious minutes she was free of the intensity of the situation and by the time she returned to the table with the drinks, Hemingway was already back.

"That was fast," she said. "I got you an Americano, too, I hope that's okay?"

He took the steaming mug with a smile. "Perfect. Thank you."

"So, how do we do this?" Elba asked.

Hem reached in his pocket and with a quick glance around the pub, pulled out the crumpled piece of paper containing the spell and the small black stone. Elba tried to ignore the small specks of blood on the yellowed sheet. "If we do it under the table, we should be okay. It's not like it's bangs and fireworks."

Elba found herself trembling with anticipation. As scary as it had been the first time, she'd quite enjoyed the tingle of power running through her.

"Do you want to link to me again, like last time?" Hem asked, his gaze flitting to Kip in question.

"Link to me," Kip said. "If you insist on putting yourself in harm's way, I'd like to know where you are if anything goes wrong."

A small spark of relief flickered in her chest. They'd discussed the way the stone had felt like a link between her and Hem. If Kip was willing to have that, maybe he hadn't written her off completely.

Hem handed Kipling the paper and placed the stone in Elba's hand. She tucked her fist under the table, where Kip's hand wrapped around it. He spoke the spell so softly, she could barely make it out. Not that she understood whatever language it was in.

Even though she couldn't see it, she could feel the symbols on the stone's surface heat against her palm and she knew if she looked, they'd be glowing. As the stone warmed, she felt the tingling sensation spreading up through her arm and across her chest. She gasped as the scar on her breast seared red hot and pulled her hand away from Kip's.

His eyes flashed with concern as they looked her over. "What is it? Are you okay?"

Elba rubbed her chest before pulling her top forward to peer down at the scar. Her eyes widened as she watched the white lines of scar tissue glow pale blue.

"My scar," she wheezed. "It's glowing."

Hem frowned. "Well, that can't be good."

Elba gaped at him. "What do you mean?"

"Maybe we should go back to the apartment and test out your magic," Kip suggested. "We can take a look at the scar, too."

Before Elba could respond, a shadow fell over the table. She looked up to find a tall, slim, brown haired man staring down at them, his ice-blue eyes taking in every detail as he looked at each of them in turn.

"I believe you wanted to speak to me."

NINE

BOTH KIP AND HEM TENSED, their hands poised as though ready to grab weapons. Elba carefully slid the conduit stone into her pocket. She could feel Kip's flames flickering under her skin, the power so much stronger than when she'd linked to Hem. This time, she realised, there was no restrictor dampening it.

"That depends," Hem said, staring up the man. "Who are you?"

"I'm Lawrence," he said. "Did I come all the way over here for nothing?"

Kip shared a look with Hem, then gestured to the last empty seat around the table. When Lawrence sat, she noticed that the pub was busier. Three men and a woman stood near the bar, glancing at them every so often. Of course, Lawrence hadn't come alone.

"I'd like to cast a screening spell around us, if that's okay?" Lawrence asked. "My people will make sure we're not disturbed, but I'd rather what is said, stays between us."

Kip nodded, his jaw tight. "Fine."

Lawrence muttered a string of words, and pale blue wisps that matched his eyes swirled around his fingers and neck, shimmering with glittered sparks. It was so pretty, Elba couldn't help but stare.

"So, you found your restrictors?" he asked as the iridescent blue mist faded.

There was an easy calm about the man—the self-assured composure of someone who knows they're in complete control. Elba knew Hemingway and Kipling could feel it too, as tension poured off them in waves.

"Look." Lawrence leaned back and folded his arms across his olive-green cable knit sweater. "I know you don't trust me, but believe me, the feeling is mutual. I've taken a huge risk coming here. For all I know, this is a trap."

"Why did you come, then?" Hem asked.

Lawrence scratched the stubble on his sharp chin, the light streaming through the window catching on flashes of auburn. "For Selena."

If Hem tensed any harder, he would explode. Elba resisted the urge to put a hand on his shoulder.

"I know she'd die before giving us up," he continued, his unusual pale blue eyes narrowing. "So, if she told you to come and see me, it means she trusts you."

"Are you the leader?" Kip asked.

Lawrence smiled and shook his head. "No. I'm not. Look, tell me why you're here. What do you want? Do you want to join the movement?"

Hem baulked and a strange noise rippled from Kip's throat. Elba stared at them both, eyes wide. The mistrust and hatred they had for the Freedoms was so ingrained, they were struggling to function.

"No," Kip said, his voice thick with disgust. "We don't want to join the movement."

Lawrence sighed. "So, what are we doing here?"

"We want answers," Hem bit out. "Why are the bureau putting restrictors in people?"

"Surely you should be asking that question to the bureau?"

Kip narrowed his eyes. "Just tell us."

"Why should I tell you anything?" Lawrence said, his eyes flashing. "How many of my people have you captured? Killed? You were told we were the enemy, and you swallowed the lie whole, without question. Now, you're sitting here, gagging for answers and you expect me to just tell you everything?"

Hem's hands clenched into fists, the tanned skin across his knuckles turning pale. "We just want to know why."

"Why what?" Lawrence asked. "Why they put restrictors in you? Or why we're fighting against them?"

"Both," Kip said.

Lawrence unfolded his arms, bracing his hands on his knees. "You already know the answer to the first question. They want you weakened."

Elba's heart thumped a steady pounding rhythm against her ribcage. She wondered whether the only thing stopping Hem and Kip from exploding was the fact she was sitting there.

After a full minute of silence, Lawrence slapped his hands down on his knees and made to stand. "Well, I suppose that's us done, then. Don't bother asking for me again. I'm not sure what Selena thought any of us would get from this."

Elba clamped her lips together. She wanted to tell him to stop—that they really were desperate for answers. This wasn't her battle, however, so she stayed quiet. Even though it killed her.

She jumped as Hem's phone buzzed where it lay on the table. He snatched it up, swearing under his breath.

"What is it?" Kip asked.

Hem's face clouded. "They're interrogating Selena again this afternoon."

Lawrence turned to them—a darkness flickering in his eyes. "They didn't get rid of her yet? I assumed . . ."

Kip's threw a glance at Hem before replying, "What do you mean?"

Lawrence slid his hands into his pockets. "If you saw the holding floor, I would have thought you'd have seen the incinerator."

"The *what*?" Hem asked, his voice strained.

"I've not seen it in person, but I've heard about it from Men who defected to us. What do you think they do with the bodies?"

Elba's stomach turned, her hand moving to her mouth. Both Kip and Hem paled. Selena's time was up.

"I'll tell you what," Lawrence said. "I'll tell you everything, if you do something for me."

"We don't work for the Freedoms," Kip said, his voice ice cold.

Elba was sure she saw Lawrence flinch at the term as he raised his dark brows. "You're still one hundred percent loyal to the bureau? Even after they stunted your magic? Even after you've found out they're planning to murder your friend? I'm assuming that's what Selena is to you. Or perhaps was, before she sought the truth."

"What do you want?" Hem asked.

"Free Selena," Lawrence replied, as though he was asking them to buy him a coffee. "Get her out and bring her to Dutting Airfield. I'll have a flight chartered to get her back to Venezuela."

Elba's eyes widened. How much money did the Freedoms have at their disposal that they could just charter flights at the drop of a hat?

Lawrence reached into his pocket and pulled out a square piece of paper no bigger than a Post It note. He placed it on the table. "If you decide to take me up on my offer, just let me know. Save Selena and I promise, I'll answer every question you have."

Kip and Hem stared at the blank piece of paper, leaving Lawrence to give her a small smile before turning and walking away. She watched as the other Freedoms filed out behind him, leaving them alone, with only the old man—possibly asleep—at the bar.

"How do we get in touch?" Elba asked, peering at the paper.

Hem picked it up, turning it over in his hands before placing it in his coat pocket. "You write on it and he'll get the message. It's basically an ancient, magical version of text messaging."

Elba blew out a slow breath. "What are you going to do?"

"If we free Selena, we're signing our own death warrants," Kip said. "We would be defying the bureau beyond explanation. There's no way we could come back from it."

Elba chewed her bottom lip, watching his pained expression and longing to kiss away the crease between his brows. "Do you want to go back?"

Hem groaned, poking at his now cold cup of coffee. "It's all we've ever known, El. That Lawrence guy is asking us to walk away from our friends. Our family."

"The family who planted restrictors in you as kids," Elba countered.

Kip frowned. "Is it any worse than putting a tracker in your kid's phone?"

"Are you serious?" Elba laughed. "You sound brainwashed. They have an actual incinerator to dispose of bodies. You do realise what that means?"

"We know exactly what it means," Kip growled.

She folded her arms. "So, what are you going to do?"

Kip smacked his fists down on the table so hard, it sent cold coffee splashing across the varnished surface. "I don't know!"

Elba stared at him, aghast. She knew his anger wasn't directed at her. She could see him crumbling before her and all she wanted to do was hold him, in the hope that it would keep him from falling apart. Her fingers twitched, aching to reach for his trembling fist, but she turned to Hemingway, tucking her hands between her legs instead.

"Would it even be possible? Can it even be done?" she asked.

Hem scratched his chin. "I could ask Eli to black out security again. I'm not sure we can trust him enough to ask him to hack into the system and unlock her door."

"Would you be able to use magic to unlock the door?"

Kip shoved back his chair and stood. "I'll be back in a minute."

Elba watched, open mouthed, as he stormed to the door. Shoving it open, he disappeared out onto the street. She turned to Hem, finding him staring after his friend, his mouth a thin line.

"Is he going to be okay?" she asked.

Hem sighed, poking at the puddle of cold coffee pooled on the table. "Yeah. It's just hitting him really hard."

"It's hitting you both hard," she said softly.

"Yeah." Hem snorted. He looked at her, sadness lining his midnight blue eyes. "Give him time."

He opened his mouth to say more but shook his head instead. Elba didn't need him to say the words. She knew what he was going to say. Kipling had never got over being given up by his parents as a child. Her heart ached as she thought of the warm Italian couple she'd met at Marco's Restaurant. The parents who didn't even remember they had another son. Now, he was at risk of losing the only family he had left.

She bit down her lip, recalling the pain in his eyes when he'd seen her in Alex's arms. Kip had said she was his lighthouse, but now he was scared she would abandon him just like everyone else.

"He won't lose us," she whispered, more to herself than Hem.

Elba could feel him staring at her and when she lifted her head to meet his gaze, he gave her a small smile and nodded towards the door. "Why don't you tell him that?"

She opened her mouth to argue but Hem just raised his eyebrows. Elba frowned and stood. There was a good chance he'd shout at her, but whatever he might say, surely it couldn't be worse than what had happened that morning. Her heart in her stomach, she pushed open the heavy door and stepped out onto the quiet street.

For a second, Elba thought he'd magicked away. But then she felt a tug on the thin, invisible string of magic linking them and turned, finding him leaning against the wall at the edge of the building. Taking a shaky breath, she walked towards him. If he heard her approach, he didn't show it—his eyes fixed on the pavement.

Any words she wanted to say scrambled to the back of her brain as she opened her mouth. "Hey."

Elba waited for him to tell her to go away, but he didn't. So, she leaned against the wall beside him. It was cold out on the street and she wrapped her arms around herself.

Standing there in silence, she tried a million different lines in her head, but when she envisioned saying them, they all resulted in Kip walking away. Perhaps she was wrong, but she wasn't quite brave enough to take the risk. Then again, if she went back inside having said nothing . . . She could picture the look Hem would give her.

Elba pushed herself off the wall and stood in front of him so that he was now staring at her shoes. "You don't have to talk to me, but I came out here to tell you something." She paused, giving him the chance to tell her to stop, but he didn't so much as move. "I know you feel like everything is falling apart, but it's not. No matter what happens, you have us—me and Hem. Push me away all you like, but I'm not going anywhere."

Elba stared at Kip's hanging head, her fingers clenching at her side as she fought the urge to reach out and cup his cheek, lift his chin. After a minute, she turned to head back inside. She'd said what she'd came to say.

She'd barely taken two steps, when a hand gripped hers, pulling her to a halt. Elba's heart hammered as she turned to find Kip watching her, tears staining his sharp cheekbones, his silver eyes shimmering like stars.

"Oh, Kip," she breathed.

No longer caring, she closed the distance between them and rose up on her toes, wrapping her arms around him. He buried his face in her neck and she stroked his hair, the other hand rubbing his back.

"I told you I was a mess," he muttered.

Elba winced at the sharp pain in her chest. Pulling back a little, she cupped his face in her hands, wiping away his tears with her thumbs. "It's okay to be a mess."

"That's what you said last time."

She raised her eyebrows. "It's still true."

He stared at her, a small frown on his face as though trying to figure something out.

"What?" she asked.

"Why bother?"

She took in his face, fighting the urge to run her thumb over his soft lips. "Bother with what?"

"Me."

Elba tried to hide the smile forming on her lips. "Other than the fact you're an incredible shag?"

Kip laughed and she felt her shoulders relax a little at the deep, rumbling sound.

"I care about you," Elba said, brushing the curls from his

forehead. "A lot. Do you really want me to go into a list of reasons of why I think you're worth it?"

Kip smiled, although it didn't fully reach his eyes. "It couldn't hurt."

Elba laughed, letting her hands fall to her sides. "I'm going to go back in. Are you coming?"

He looked away, the frown forming between his brows once more.

"Well, whenever you're ready." As an afterthought, she rose up on her tiptoes and leaned forward to press a kiss to his cheek.

Her lips had barely left his chilled skin when he turned his face and caught her mouth with his. Elba jolted with surprise and as he pulled back, she saw something flash in his eyes that made her breath catch in her throat.

Before she could question it, he leaned forward and claimed her mouth again. It was not a gentle kiss as his hand slid into her hair, the other gripping the back of her neck as he forcefully swept her mouth with his tongue.

Elba's hands found his waist, her cold fingers sliding under his soft blue sweater, grazing the taut skin beneath. Kip inhaled at the touch, spinning them around and pushing her up against the wall. She whimpered as he pressed his hard body against her, breaking the kiss only long enough to bite her lip.

Elba ran her hands up and down his body, her fingers snagging on the ridges of his abs. She trailed her fingertips along the waistband of his jeans, and he moaned against her lips, nudging her legs apart as he ground against her.

How far was this going to go? Part of her screamed to stop —that they were out on the street—but she was so lost in the desperation of his kisses, she found herself sliding her hands down the back of his jeans and pressing him closer. Beneath her skin, magic thrummed and pulsed as though reaching out to mesh with Kip's. A low rumbling noise sounded in his throat and he broke the kiss, his chest rising and falling fast. Elba opened her eyes, her swollen lips suddenly cold in the absence of his mouth.

Kip grabbed hold of her wrist and pulled her around the corner of the building. As soon as they were ensconced in shadow, Elba expected to be swallowed by silver flames. Instead, he pinned her against the wall again. Grabbing a fistful of her hair, he tugged her head backwards, scraping his teeth along her jaw, her neck, her collar bone. Elba moaned and he tightened the grip on her hair, pressing himself against her again as his other hand reached under her sweater, teasing her nipple through her bra. She gasped and Kip's mouth found hers again—a desperate clash of teeth and tongues that stole her breath. He let her hair fall from his fingers, his hands trailing down her body and Elba reached up and wound her hands in his curls.

Kip pulled back, breathing hard, his eyes dark with a wildness that caused her heart to slam against her ribcage. He tugged her to a stack of empty wooden crates and lifted her up onto one. The giggle rising in her throat at being almost eye to eye died on her lips as Kip's fingers began unfastening her jeans.

Elba gasped, as he turned her around, tugging them down to her thighs along with her underwear. One hand pressed her against his chest, massaging her breast as the other slid between her legs. His teeth tugged at her earlobe as his fingers pushed inside her. Elba leaned her head back against his shoulder, his touch drawing small gasps of pleasure as she felt his magic roil around her. Or was it inside her? Heady with desire, she was too lost to care.

He withdrew his hand and Elba whimpered, but the sound of his fly unzipping halted the protest in her throat. Kip dragged his teeth against her neck as he gripped her hair again, pulling her back against him. When she felt his hard length against her, she pushed back against him, desperate with need for him. His grip tightened on her hair, his teeth on her collarbone as he entered her with a single commanding thrust.

No longer caring whether anyone heard, Elba cried out. Kip turned her head, claiming her mouth as he pulled almost all the way out before slamming into her again. Elba whimpered, reaching out to brace herself against the brick wall. Kip wrapped a muscled arm across her chest, his other hand massaging her clit as he claimed her again and again with a ferocity and need, she hadn't experienced from him before.

His fingers stroked and teased between her legs as he pounded into her, her whimpers turned to gasps as she came, tightening around him. He swore under his breath pressing her against his chest as flames licked at his skin. Kip gripped her chin, turning her face to his and swallowing her moans as she shuddered against him.

When their breathing returned to normal, Kip pulled out and slid her jeans back up. Despite what they'd just done, Elba's stomach filled with nerves as she prepared to turn and face him. He'd said he wanted to cool things off a bit, but what had just happened was anything but that.

Drawing a tentative breath, she turned around. Kip smoothed his hair and straightened his clothes before meeting her gaze.

"Are you okay?" he asked, a flicker of worry on his face.

Elba realised she could easily cry. Not because of what had just happened, but because all she wanted to do was wrap her arms around his neck and hold him, but she didn't know if she was allowed.

"Are *you* okay?" she asked.

He gave her a sheepish smile and ran a hand through his hair. "Yeah. I just . . ." He shook his head and reached to touch her but dropped his hand. "I can't think straight when you're near me."

Elba stared at him, her gaze falling on his swollen lips. "I need to know," she said, willing her voice not to tremble. "Was that just you getting out some frustration? Do you still want to cool things down?"

Kip opened his mouth, but shut it again, pressing his lips together until the colour receded—the crease between his brows appearing once more.

Biting down on her lip, Elba stepped down off the crate. "Let's go back inside."

It took every ounce of strength she had not to cry as she stalked back to the pub, the pull of the magic linking them feeling like some sort of twisted joke. Elba plastered a smile on her face as she shoved open the door, not bothering to hold it open for Kip behind her.

Hem looked up as they approached, his phone in his hand. "Eli says he can do it," he said. "We've got two hours to figure out how the fuck we're going to pull this off."

TEN

"LIKE I SAID, if we do it, we're crossing a line," Kip said, pacing in front of the window in Hemingway's apartment. "There's no coming back from this."

"If we don't do it, there's no coming back for Selena," Hem countered, tapping a pen against his knee. "It's pretty cut and dry. We risk our necks to save her life and get some answers, or we let her die and stay in the fucking dark. I know which one I choose."

Kip stopped pacing and stared at him, his expression dark. "It's far from cut and dry."

"It really isn't," Hem said. "All you have to do is pick a side."

Elba tried to tune out their bickering, focusing instead on her fingers. She could feel Kipling's silver flames under her skin, rippling like long grass in a breeze. Last time, when she'd linked to Hem's power, she'd had to focus on anger to push the bursts of power out. This time, the overriding emotion was likely to be fear. She would have to figure out a way to control the power with more precision and she was running out of time.

"There's no way a simple spell will work on the doors,"

Kip snapped. "If we get down there and the glass is too heavily warded, we'll run out of time, the cameras will come back on and we'll be exposed. I don't know about you, but I really don't fancy spending any time on the other side of those cells."

"Why would it be heavily warded, though?" Hem reasoned. "The prisoners are covered in restrictors and no one knows they're down there."

"Lawrence knew," Kip said, his jaw ticking.

Hem leaned back against the sofa with a sigh. "He knows the place exists. He doesn't know where it is, and he doesn't have an Eli to black it out."

Kip made a noise that sounded a lot like a snarl at the mention of the redhead's name. "What does that prick want in return for all this?"

"'That 'prick' is risking his neck so we can say goodbye to our friend," Hem replied. "He's going to get in deep shit when we pull a prison break."

Elba frowned, willing the flickering feeling underneath her skin upwards, trying to visualise it. When nothing happened, she huffed and clenched her fist.

"You're trying too hard," Hem said, looking over at her. "You'll blow a blood vessel the way you're doing it."

Elba shot him a withering look. "What should I do, then? I haven't been able to use the magic without a spell other than when I'm angry."

The corner of Hem's mouth twitched. "I'm sure if you think hard enough you can think of a reason to be angry."

Kip flipped him off between pacing and Hem laughed.

"Tell me what to do," Elba said, purposefully ignoring Kip. It was easy enough to ignore his pacing, but it was a lot harder to ignore the fine string of power linking them.

"Close your eyes and picture it," Hem said, taking her hand and unfurling her fist. "Don't push the power outwards. Command it. Tell it where to go."

Elba pulled a face. "Command it?"

"Yep. In your head. Show it who's boss."

Staring at her open palm, Elba imagined the silver flames, lined with flecks of gold, flickering and licking at her skin. She tried not to think about the way they danced over Kip's bare skin or the way he commanded the gentle flames to tease her body. Shaking her head, she concentrated and barked the order in her head to the shimmering power beneath her skin.

Flames lit up around her hand like a gas stove and she squealed in delight. "I did it!"

"There you go," Hem said, squeezing her knee. "Easy."

She turned over her hand and flexing her fingers between the sparks, mesmerised by the way they gleamed, tickling her skin. "It's so beautiful . . ." she whispered.

"Try and send the magic out," Hem said. "Like before."

He didn't need to say any more. The last time they'd practised this, Kip had been with Naomi and Selena, being carved to pieces. Elba nodded, focusing her attention on a baseball cap on the high table near the door. Once again, instead of pushing, she envisioned what she wanted the power to do and willed it to shoot out and sweep the cap to the floor.

The flames roared out from her fingertips, but they didn't knock the hat to the floor. Instead, they surrounded it, turning red and gold as it burst into flame.

"Shit!" Hem yelped, leaping to his feet.

Elba watched, eyes wide as he conjured water from thin air, dousing the hat and sending keys, receipts and what looked like sweet wrappers, to the floor in a wave.

"I'm so sorry," she gasped, her eyes wide as the remains of the hat sizzled in the pool of water.

Hem shook his head. "I suppose it's stronger now we've not got the restrictors in. I didn't think about how different Kip's power is to mine either." He turned to his friend, who had paused his pacing to watch them. "Perhaps it should be you giving your girlfriend magic lessons."

Elba winced at the word, staring at the puddle on the carpet, the sofa, her feet—anywhere but Kipling.

Hem groaned. "What the fuck is going on between you two?"

"Let me fetch a cloth," Elba said, heading to the kitchen.

"Wait." Hem looked between them, his eyes wide. "Did you two break up?"

Elba forced herself to keep walking to the kitchen, blood roaring in her ears. She certainly wasn't going to answer Hem's question, but she couldn't help but hope that Kip would.

"We need to concentrate on planning this rescue," Kip said, his words clipped.

Elba exhaled and grabbed a couple of tea towels before heading back to the mess she'd made. She'd barely stooped for the puddle when Hem put out a hand to stop her.

"No. Sorry guys. We're not avoiding this." He looked between them, his expression fierce. "In less than an hour, we're going into a potentially life-threatening situation. I'm not doing that with a pair of sulky teenagers."

Elba gasped. "I am not—"

Hem silenced her with a look before turning to Kip. "Did you break up with Elba? Did you seriously only make it two days? Was it even that? What the fuck?"

Elba cringed, putting out a hand to stop him, but he shook her off.

"No, Elba. He needs to hear this." He folded his arms across his broad chest. "Kip, mate. You need to sort yourself out. I've never seen you as fucking smitten as you are with Elba. I've never seen you smitten, full stop. Why are you trying so hard to fuck it up?"

"Leave it." Kip's voice was ice.

Elba finally let herself look at him and she froze. He stood, rigid, flames rippling at his fingertips as he glared at Hemingway.

"No, I won't," Hem said. "You're being a self-destructive prick and you know damn well I'll always call you out on that sort of bullshit behaviour."

Kip's gaze flitted to her for a second and she realised she was barely breathing. Her heart was torn. Half of her wanted to end it herself. What he was doing to her wasn't fair and she hated being a trembling mess. The other half of her knew that running away from him was exactly what he was expecting.

He'd never pretended to be anything other than a mess and she'd taken him on more than willingly. If she could get him to let her in—to see that she was in this for the long haul —then it would be worth it. She just hadn't thought it would be so hard to get him to believe in her—in them.

"We haven't broken up," Kip muttered, his eyes fixed on the floor.

Elba looked up, her heart leaping.

"Why does Elba look so surprised to hear that, then?" Hem asked, giving her a look that threatened to bring tears to the surface.

Her cheeks heated and, even though she wished she knew how to magic herself back to her own apartment, she forced herself to look at Kip. She barely had time to take in the broken look on his face before he was striding across the room towards her. He pulled her into his arms, holding her tight enough that she could hear his heartbeat through his shirt.

"I'm sorry El," he whispered. "I didn't mean to make you think I wanted to end things. My head's just such a mess . . ." He pulled back enough to look at her, his eyes filled with apology. "I understand if you want to run. I won't stop you."

Elba groaned, bracing her hands against his chest. "That's just it, Kip. I don't want to run, and even if I did, I'd want you to try and stop me. I want to fight for us. I want you to fight for us." She drew a shaky breath, gathering the words that had been forming in her heart since sitting and waiting in the bar that morning. "I'm in. Mess and all. If you're not, though. If you're not even willing to try . . . I don't know if I'm strong enough to carry both of us."

Kip stared down at her, fear shimmering in his silver-grey eyes. Elba knew her words would be an easy out for him—an excuse to run for the hills. She braced herself for the step back, for the absence of his touch, but he reached out and cupped her face instead.

"I want to try," he said. "I am trying. The fact you're even still here after how I've behaved today . . ." He shook his head. "I don't deserve you."

Elba sighed and reached up to touch his face. "That's just the thing, Kip. You do. You do deserve me. You deserve happiness."

He frowned and as she reached up to smooth it away, he leaned his head against hers. "Thank you for not giving up on me."

"I hope you two are going to start paying me for these counselling sessions," Hem said from where he was sending spirals of smoke to clean up the mess of water and scorch marks.

Elba tutted. "Why didn't you say you could use magic to clean it up?"

Hem shrugged, the grin on his face masking something more serious underneath. "You didn't ask."

Elba stepped away from Kip and wrapped her arms around him. "Thank you."

"It needed to be cleaned up anyway," he said, squeezing her tight.

She pinched his shoulder. "You know exactly what I'm talking about."

"Yeah, well, you just need to call him out on it," Hem said, pressing a kiss to her cheek before shaking his head at Kip. "He may look like a kicked puppy, but he can take it."

Kip pulled a face before holding out a hand for Elba. She

felt a thousand times lighter as he pulled her back against his chest, pressing a kiss to the top of her head. "What are we going to do about Selena? We're running out of time."

"I actually think I might have an idea," Elba said. "If you think you won't be able to get into her cell, why not wait until she's not in the cell?"

Hem gave a murmur of approval. "That could work. If we ambush them when they're taking her to the interrogation—"

"We could knock them out and run," Kip finished. "There's no way we could get back up the elevator and out through the front doors with Selena, though."

Elba frowned. Of course. The bureau was warded against people magicking in and out. As soon as they saw Selena, they'd be stopped. Her breath caught in her throat and she tightened her grip on Kip's arms.

"What if they couldn't see her?" She gasped.

Kip tilted his head to look at her. "What do you mean?"

"What if you made Selena invisible?" she explained. "She could walk right out of there."

Hem shook his head. "There are wards for that. It's why we made you invisible once we got to Kip's office."

"When would the wards alert people?" Elba asked.

Hem's eyes widened. "When she tries to leave."

The reality of the situation settled over them in heavy silence. When they left with an invisible Selena, the wards would be triggered, and the bureau would come after them. Of course, once they were outside the doors, they could magic away. That wasn't the problem, though. The bureau would know it was them. Then, there really would be no way back.

ELEVEN

IF ELBA THOUGHT WALKING through the security arch in the lobby had been stressful the day before, this was a whole other level. Her heart slammed against her chest as they moved towards the pale stone archway. There was no queue today. Perhaps because it was Sunday, or perhaps because it was mid-afternoon, and more people were leaving than arriving.

None of them were sure what would happen when the conduit stone passed through the arch. Kip had cast a cloaking spell around it and Hem had found a small black velvet pouch warded with cloaking spells to put the stone in. Whether it would work or not, none of them knew. The plan was, if the stone set off the arch, they would say they were turning it in as evidence. They might even have to do so; but it would be better than the other option.

Staring up at the arch, Elba willed her face into something she hoped was neutral. Carl wasn't on duty today. A painfully thin man with a hooked nose and large eyebrows squinted at her instead as he held out the tray for her personal belongings. Elba made a show of patting her pockets and pulling out her phone and keys—the stone safely tucked away in her bra.

Just as last time, Hem had already passed through. Behind her, Kip fished his own phone from his pockets, making polite conversation with the guard. Elba couldn't focus on their words though, instead concentrating on her breathing as she stepped through the archway. Kip's magic ebbed and flowed in her veins, stroking the underside of her skin as though alive. She couldn't help but wonder whether it did the same for him or whether he was controlling it somehow. There was still so much they didn't know about how the conduit stone worked.

Above her, the arch glowed and hummed—its magic surrounding and probing her. Could it tell she wasn't supposed to have magic? Could it tell she was a wielder? Elba kept her eyes on Hemingway, who smiled at her, his hands casually in his jeans pockets as though they were just popping into the office to pick something up.

When the arch glowed white in approval, Elba's legs quaked as she stepped forward. She didn't dare look at the others as she collected her belongings, instead focusing on her phone as they made their way to the elevator. They rode up in silence. The last thing they wanted to do was cause anyone to look their way. Normal was the name of the game. Mundane, even.

By the time they opened the door to Kip's office, Elba was trembling. She sank down onto the sofa, wringing her hands as Kip cast a spell around the room to ensure they could talk freely.

"Eli says they're interrogating her at four," Hem said, staring at his phone.

Elba glanced at her watch. It was twenty to. "Has he questioned you about it?"

"No." Hem's mouth thinned.

Eli was willing to black out the cameras like last time, and

Hem had asked him to do it from quarter to four, on the promise they would be done quickly and out before someone came to take Selena to her interrogation.

It had been a difficult moment of realisation. There was no way of rescuing Selena without revealing themselves to the bureau. Elba reached out and touched Kip's hand where he stood, statue-still, beside her. The last seventeen years of their lives had been spent with the bureau and today they would blow it all up. He stroked a finger along hers, but remained rigid, staring out the window at the sprawling city beyond.

Elba looked between the two of them, almost green with nausea at the thought of what lay ahead. Eli would black out the cameras and they'd descend, unseen, to the secret floor, but they wouldn't be leaving under the cover of darkness.

"What if they stop the elevator?" Elba whispered. "How fast can they do that?"

Kip rolled his neck. "Speed is key. They won't be expecting this."

His words didn't calm Elba's nerves and, as he turned and cast the spell to turn her invisible, her heart thundered even louder.

Hem smoothed his hair back, tying it tighter, as though preparing to head into battle. "It's time."

With every step towards the secret elevator, Elba thought she might vomit. She tried to concentrate on her role, reciting the spells she'd learnt over and over in her head. After the warehouse, the words of those spells would be forever etched in her memory, but she repeated them, nonetheless.

The descent seemed faster this time, the doors opening to the dark corridor before Elba had time to prepare herself. They strode past the row of glass walls and she tried not to look at the prisoners on the other side—the ones they would not be saving today.

When they came to a stop outside Selena's cell, Elba sucked in a sharp breath. Slumped in the corner, eyes closed, she looked awful. Perhaps anticipating her death today, they hadn't given her any medical attention and her wounds were angry and swollen, her face blue tinged. Her dark hair was still matted with blood and the front of her grey sweats was stained dark. Elba's eyes burned and she turned away, sucking in steading breaths to stem the vomit from rising.

"Selena?" Hem hissed. "Hey."

Elba heard a faint shuffle and forced herself to turn around. Selena's brow furrowed at the sight of them.

"Why are you here?" she rasped.

"We're going to get you out," Hem said.

Selena's dark eyes widened, the disbelief and hope that flashed in their beaten depths enough to cause Elba to press a hand to the wall to steady herself.

"They're coming to take you for another round in a few minutes," Kip said, glancing back at the elevator. "When they do, we're going to take them out."

"We'll cast an invisibility spell and we're going to walk right out the front door," Hem finished.

Selena laughed. At least, it started as a laugh, but ended as a painful, hacking cough. "There's no way that will work."

"We can leave you to die, if you'd prefer?" Kip said, his voice cold. "Maybe I'll stand by and watch them kill you, like you did to me."

The smile faded from Selena's lips. "I'm so sorry, Kip. I would never have let her kill you. I'd have found a way. You have to believe me."

Kip shook his head and turned away as Hem explained the rest of the plan. Elba reached out and pressed an invisible hand to his chest. He placed his hand over the top, pressing it to his heart.

"It's time," Hem said.

Both he and Kip muttered the now familiar wording that caused them to ripple into nothingness. It was a strange sensation, being invisible, surrounded by invisible people.

Elba's hand was still on Kip's chest and she stroked the warm, hard plane now, marvelling at how she could see her own hand, yet it looked as though she was touching thin air.

Kip's hand took hold of hers, the other tracing down her arm, up her shoulder until it found her neck. His fingers slid up the sensitive skin until they reached her face. As he cupped her cheek, she leaned into his touch, closing her eyes.

The elevator doors slid open at the end of the corridor and Elba stifled a gasp. It wasn't the same Men who interrogated Selena before. This time, it was two men she hadn't seen before. They strode down the corridor, their faces set in frowns. Perhaps they knew what they would be doing after the interrogation. At the thought, Elba glanced at the end of the corridor they hadn't been, looking for the incinerator Lawrence had promised was there.

Just as the beginnings of relief began to set in that perhaps it wasn't there after all, she saw it. At the end of the corridor, on the left-hand wall, a large square metal hatch was fixed into the wall. It might have been something else, but a dark feeling in her gut told her it was what she dreaded.

Elba pressed herself against the far wall as the two Men reached Selena's cell. She couldn't feel or see Kip or Hem, but she assumed they were pressed along the wall beside her. One of the Men flipped down a control panel covering she hadn't noticed built into the side of the wall and typed in a six-digit code. Elba couldn't help a swell of disappointment. She'd assumed the cells were locked with a combination of powerful magic.

One of the Men stepped back as the door to the cell glowed red and the other pulled out a knife. Elba's mouth fell open. Were they really just going to kill Selena right here? As she watched, however, he took the knife and sliced across the back of his forearm. Turning the wound, he let the blood drip to the floor outside the door. Elba stared, entranced, as the red glow of the door faded, and it clicked open. A keypad and blood magic—the best of both worlds, she supposed.

The Men strode in and grabbed Selena's arms, dragging her to her feet. She cried out in pain and Elba winced, remembering that her injuries from the day before most likely included broken bones. They hadn't really considered her not being able to walk out. Her feet dragging on the floor alongside her whimpers of pain, the Men pulled her through the door, and it sealed behind them.

Elba couldn't see them but she heard the scuffle of feet and smelt the scents of their magic as Kip and Hem launched at the two Men. Completely taken by surprise, they had no chance to react before a mixture of fists and magic reduced them to crumpled heaps. Elba rushed forward to catch Selena as she fell with them, unable to hold herself up.

Although not much taller than Elba, Selena was a solid mass of muscle and she sagged under her weight. "You're going to be okay," she whispered as Selena groaned against her.

A flicker of surprise flashed across her bruised and battered face and Elba realised Selena wouldn't have known she was there.

Somewhere nearby, Kipling whispered the invisibility spell and Selena's bloodied form disappeared, leaving only her laboured breathing in her ear and her dead weight against her.

"Let's go," Hem hissed.

"Do the guards as well," Elba whispered. "Make them invisible, too. It might buy us some time."

After a pause, Kip whispered the spell again and the unconscious guards disappeared. If anyone looked at the cameras, they'd see an empty corridor. It was a slim chance that no one had noticed the two guards being attacked, but they could use any chance they could get.

Hem felt for her, lifting Selena from her arms, and they

sprinted towards the elevator. Someone reached out and smacked the button repeatedly, as though it might make the doors open sooner.

Elba's heart thrashed against her chest with such ferocity she thought she might vomit. Whatever cameras were hidden in the dark recesses of the ceiling were watching now—even if they couldn't see them.

They stepped into the elevator, the sound of their ragged breathing almost deafening alongside Selena's moans.

"We'll never make it," she groaned.

Hem shushed her. "Not with that attitude we won't."

The scent of woodsmoke filled the small space and Selena gasped as his magic healed her. Elba had no idea how much Hem was able to heal, but by the time the elevator doors slid open, the rasp in Selena's breath had eased.

They walked quickly down the corridor, past the rows of black doors with their gold name plates. Elba tried not to think about how many Men would be behind those doors. Perhaps not many with it being late on a Sunday afternoon.

As they passed Hem's door, a pang of sadness caused Elba to swallow. They wouldn't be able to come back here, Kip and Hem. There was nothing in Kip's office, but Hem's was filled with memories and personal affects. He'd have to leave them all behind. Elba wondered whether he had considered this—whether he cared.

They reached the elevator, and someone pressed the button. Tears burned in Elba's eyes. She could hardly draw a breath as her body pulsed with nerves. At some point an alarm would be raised. She had no idea what that would look like in a place like this—a place of magic. Would spells keep them in place? Would people appear around them out of nowhere?

Elba thought of herself in one of those cells, bloodied, beaten and soiled awaiting her turn in the incinerator, and a small whimper escaped her lips. She'd been an idiot. She shouldn't have come. Closing her eyes, she drew in a shaky breath and tried to calm her erratic heart. If she hadn't come, she would have been pacing back and forth scared out of her mind that Kip and Hem had been captured or killed. If they were, she'd never know. Would that be worse?

A hand touched her back, feeling until it slid down her arm. Warm fingers encased hers and squeezed. She glanced down at her curled hand, feeling Kip's fingers stroke against her linking ring. Elba wondered if it was on purpose. How much of her terror he was feeling right now on top of his own? A ripple of guilt washed through her and she attempted a small smile, even though she knew Kip couldn't see. She would try and pull it together, for both their sakes. His hand fell from hers as the elevator doors opened and they stepped inside.

What would be waiting for them when the doors opened on the ground floor? Elba pressed her lips together to keep in the squeaks of terror trying to escape. She needed to say calm. Instead, she focused on the ripples of magic underneath her skin, pulling at them, ready to send the power out if needed.

The ding as they reached the ground floor seemed so loud, Elba almost jumped out of her skin. When the doors slid open, they paused, barely breathing as they scanned the lobby. Watching. Waiting.

There was no turning back now. The large glass doors at the far end of sprawling atrium seemed miles away as they stepped out on to the polished marble floor. A handful of people milled about, seemingly unaware of the four invisible people in their midst. Elba turned to the towering archway, the same guard as before, watching with his dark eyes as someone passed beneath it.

They moved forward as one. Even though she couldn't see them, she could feel the warmth of them beside her alongside Selena's faint groans. The string of magic connecting her to Kip told her that he was on her left. They moved slowly, trying to walk as quietly as possible. Perhaps it would have been easier if it was busier—louder—to hide their footsteps.

As they made it a few meters away from the entrance, Elba's terror began to merge into elation. They were going to do it. The element of surprise had been the key. No one had been expecting them to break her out. The bureau had been overconfident and now it would pay for that mistake. A smile crept onto her face as she saw the street on the other side of the door. Freedom.

It felt like walking through a spiderweb. Elba blinked, brushing the sticky feeling from her face even as she heard Kip swear under his breath. She looked up to him in confusion, what had just happened? It was then she realised. She could see him. She could see Hem. She could see Selena, half draped across his shoulders, covered in blood. Everyone could see them.

A deafening high-pitched whine filled the air as heavy metal shutters began to fall across the tall windows and doors.

"Run!" Kip yelled.

Elba turned and raced to the doors, aware of the metal shutter slamming down towards her. She knew the door would be locked. This was pointless. They would be trapped. Panic pulsed inside her and before she could question the decision, she pulled her power forward and sent waves of silver flame out towards the nearest door, focusing on the glass panel. Beside her, she saw Kip raise his hand doing the same.

They were barely two metres from the door when the glass shattered into a million pieces, coating the floor with crystalline shards. Kip barrelled through first, reaching and grabbing Elba's hand as silver flames engulfed them, and the floor dropped away beneath their feet.

Elba screwed her eyes tight, clutching at Kip's hand as his

magic tore at her outstretched limbs and ripped at her skin, whipping her short, dark hair around her face.

When the ground solidified under their feet again, they were in an alleyway only a few streets away, the taxi they'd ordered waiting right in front of them—their getaway car. Hem and Selena materialised beside them and Kip raced to the taxi, pulling open the back door for Hem and Selena, who dived headfirst onto the seat, despite the yell of protest from the driver.

Kip launched himself into the front seat as Elba slid in beside Selena and slammed the door closed.

"Dutting Airfield," Kip barked. "Now!"

The taxi driver hesitated, but as Hem slammed his hand against the back of his seat with a growl, fear seemed to take over and he pushed the car out into traffic, speeding away. Elba watched out the window thinking that no matter how fast or far they went, it might never be enough.

TWELVE

"WHAT WAS THAT?" she asked, tearing her eyes away from the window.

"Go as fast as you can and I'll pay you triple," Kip said, his eyes fixed on the side mirror as though expecting people to appear behind them.

"It must be some sort of detector," Hem said, black smoke rippling from his fingers as he tried to heal more of Selena's wounds. "It stripped all the magic away as we walked through it."

"Is it always there?" Elba asked.

Hem glanced at her, his eyes dark. "I have no idea. I've never tried to leave like that before. It might always be there, or it might be part of their increased security."

"Why?" Selena croaked from between them. Her voice sounded like sandpaper and Elba wondered when was the last time she'd had food or drink.

"You can thank Lawrence," Kip said.

Selena's eyes widened. "You met him?"

"Yes."

Elba returned her attention to the road behind them.

Despite the terrified glances the driver was giving them, he wove in and out of the traffic putting distance between them at just enough speed to not draw attention from police.

"Will they chase us?" she asked.

Kip turned around in his seat, his gaze flickering over Selena before landing on Elba. "Doubtful. They know it was us. They're likely rooting through our offices as we speak."

Elba couldn't help but glance at Hem at the thought and found his brow furrowed and his jaw set as he pulled his magic back in and slumped against the seat.

"Where are we going?" Selena rasped.

Hem muttered something under his breath, a bottle of water appearing in his hand moments later. He handed to her, watching as she unscrewed the lid and gulped it down. "Lawrence has chartered you a flight home."

"What? Really?" She spluttered, wiping her mouth with the back of her hand.

"I called your family to warn them," Hem continued. "You can imagine how confused they were. I don't know whether they listened, but you can explain things to them yourself when you get home."

"Do you know how they dampened your magic?" Kip asked.

Elba frowned, turning to Selena. It hadn't crossed her mind that she wasn't handcuffed like before. She'd assumed that because she was so weak and broken, they hadn't thought it necessary. Of course, if her magic wasn't being stopped somehow, she could have healed herself.

"They have a solution," she said with a scowl. "They inject you with it. It burns like hell."

Hem swore. "Does it wear off?"

Selena gave him a wry smile. "I hope so."

They continued the rest of the journey in silence and Elba stared out the window, watching as the city melted away into villages and fields. The airfield was so small, she almost missed it. The road turned onto a dirt track which jolted them from side to side as it let them through the dips and bumps toward a sprawling corrugated iron building.

Elba's eyes widened at the sight of the small white plane waiting on the narrow airstrip.

"Thank you," Selena said, her eyes fixed and glistening as they took in the sight before them. "After everything, I . . ."

Hem looked away, staring out the window. "Even after everything, we wouldn't have let you die."

Selena reached out and took his hand, squeezing it between hers until he turned to look at her. "I'm sorry things happened the way they did. You deserve so much better."

Hem's eyes flickered with unspoken words, but he returned his gaze to the awaiting plane instead.

The driver pulled the taxi to a stop and Elba couldn't help but notice that he looked a little green, his hand trembling as he pulled on the brake. Kip reached out and placed a hand on the man's forearm, silver flames rippling across his skin.

When he removed his hand a moment later, he plastered a smile on his face and handed the man a wad of cash. "Thanks for the ride. It was nice to meet you. Have a great day."

The driver blinked, a bemused smile on his face as he looked between Kip and the money clutched in his fist. Elba opened her door and stepped out into the chilled air. It was for the best that the driver didn't remember, not just to protect him from the danger they'd put him in, but for his own sanity.

Hem opened his door and Selena edged out behind him with a groan. The taxi drove away, and they watched it leave, the silence it left in its wake deafening.

"Any chance you could do one last favour?" she asked, staring down at her bloodied and soiled sweats with a grimace.

Hem rolled his eyes, a ghost of a smile playing on his lips as he murmured under his breath. Selena's outfit transformed instantly into pale blue jeans and a long soft pink sweater.

"My favourite outfit!" She gasped, touching the material, her face lighting up. Then the smile faded, her eyes filling with tears as she looked at Hem.

Hem shrugged and started toward the plane, Kip falling in beside him. "Come on."

Selena watched him for a second before glancing at Elba. Elba swallowed at emotion in the beautiful woman's dark brown eyes. She didn't need to say anything. Hemingway had remembered her favourite outfit after all this time. Had conjured it knowing it would comfort her on her long journey home. He could have quite easily given her a clean version of what she'd been wearing. Elba gave her a sad smile and followed after them.

Lawrence wasn't there. Instead, a woman they'd never seen before stood at the bottom of the small steps leading up to the plane, another man and two women wearing boiler suits and hi-vis jackets standing a little behind her.

"Selena?" she asked.

Selena nodded. "That's me."

The woman gestured to the steps. "We'll depart as soon as you're on board."

Selena grasped the railing, turning to them. "Thank you," she said. "I'll never be able to repay you for what you've done."

"Stay safe," Kip said. "That's how you can repay us. Don't let us have saved your ass for nothing."

Selena smiled, what looked like a glimmer of relief crossing her face. It was the most Kip had said to her and Elba could tell the guilt of what she'd allowed to happen to him weighed heavily on her.

"Have a good life, Selena," Hem said.

Selena looked at each of them, her long dark hair twisting in the wind as she began to climb the steps up to the plane. As soon as she stepped inside, the man and woman in hi-vis jackets moved forward and pulled the stairs away, pushing them towards the building.

The woman gave them a nod. "Lawrence will be in touch soon. You still have the paper?"

Hem patted his pocket. "Yes."

Without a word, a twist of green mist wrapped around the woman and she disappeared, leaving them standing alone on the runway beside the plane. The engines started and they turned, jogging backwards to the stretch of grass alongside the tarmac.

"We did it," Kip said, as the plane began to crawl down the runway.

"We did it," Hem echoed.

"I hope the answers are worth it."

Elba looked up at Kip, his eyes narrowed as he watched the plane gather speed. "They will be. The truth is always worth it."

The whine of the plane's engines intensified as it finally lifted into the air, and they watched it until it was no more than a faint white speck amongst the clouds. Perhaps it was because none of them wanted to face what they needed to do next.

Elba shivered as a cold gust of wind swept around them and Kip shrugged off his leather jacket, wrapping it around her. She glanced up at him in thanks, inhaling his delicious scent as she savoured the warmth.

"I guess there's no putting it off anymore," Hem said, shoving his hands in his pockets. "We need to go."

"Meet you there," Kip said, nodding at his friend as he wrapped his arms around Elba.

Flames enveloped them once more and Elba closed her

eyes, burying her face against Kip's chest until they materialised in an alley beside a cheap hotel on the outskirts of the city. Hem had beaten them there and was already striding out of the alley and around the corner to the front door.

"Are you okay?" Elba asked, realising that Kip hadn't moved yet, his arms still holding her tight.

He blinked, looking down at her. "No. I'm not okay."

"You will be," she said, reaching up to touch his face. "We did the right thing. I'm sure of it."

Kip pressed his lips together, his brow furrowing. "I know."

"Come on," Elba said, stepping back out of his arms and taking his hand in hers. "Let's get out of the cold."

Kip let her lead him out of the alley and into the lobby of the ramshackle hotel. Hem leaned against the reception desk, poking at a stack of brochures for attractions in the city.

"Hello?" he called. "Anyone back there?"

After a moment, a young girl appeared, surprise on her face as she took in the three of them. Whether it was surprise at seeing anyone in general or the surprise at the two gorgeous men so out of place in the dilapidated reception, Elba couldn't tell.

"Can I help you?" she asked, her pale eyes wide as she tucked her poker straight mousey hair behind her ears.

"Yes, you can," Hem leaned closer, peering at her name tag, "Charlotte. We need two rooms please." He turned and glanced at Kip and Elba. "I'm assuming you guys want your own room?"

Kip flipped him off and Hem laughed. The girl behind the reception desk gawped at them before tapping at a computer and shoving a form across the counter for Hem to fill in.

"Do you want to share a room?" Kip whispered at her ear. "Sorry, I should have asked first."

Elba looked up at him, a smile on her lips at his worried expression. "Yes. I'm okay with sharing a room."

He stared down at her, the intensity in his silver eyes halting the breath in her throat. She'd always been drawn to him, but with the shared magic pulsing between them, it was a battle not to press herself against him, her body crying out to touch his. Kip reached out, his fingers grazing her wrist as he held her gaze. She wondered if he felt it too. Everything between them felt like a barrier she wanted to rip away. Their clothes. The air itself. The need to be against him, breathing him in, touching him was almost suffocating.

Hem coughed loudly and she blinked, breaking their stare to find him dangling a key in front of them. "You two okay?" he asked. "Should I request a room on the other side of the hotel?"

Elba's cheeks flushed, which caused Hem's grin to widen.

The hotel was so small there were no elevators, and they took the steps that would take them to rooms twenty-five and twenty-three on the second floor. The carpet was the thick, offensive paisley pattern usually found in pubs and the air smelled like stale cigarette smoke despite the signs claiming that the rooms were non-smoking.

"We need to get some supplies," Kip said as they stared at the faded stickers on the doors, looking for their rooms. "The bureau will ransack our apartments soon."

"How do you know they haven't already?" Elba asked, wincing as she remembered the state of her apartment after Selena and Naomi had searched it.

"The wards," Kip explained. "They haven't been breached yet."

"Which is weird in itself," Hem muttered. He pulled his phone out of his pocket, the screen dark. They'd all switched them off and had no plans to turn them on again any time soon. She wondered how many messages they would have from Eli alone.

"We should get stuff quickly, then," Kip said as they came to a stop outside their rooms. "Before we miss our chance."

He handed Elba the room key and before she could open her mouth to protest, he vanished in a lick of flames. She stared in horror as Hem shrugged and vanished in a cloud of black smoke leaving her standing alone in the empty hotel corridor.

THIRTEEN

ELBA CHECKED her watch for the thirtieth time. It had been eleven minutes since Kip had disappeared and she was going out of her mind with worry. The string of magic between them still hummed faintly. At least she knew he was still alive.

What if the bureau had been waiting for them? She tried not to think about what the bureau would do if they caught them. She'd have no way of knowing. Perhaps she could seek out Lawrence. After all, she'd helped Selena escape. Maybe he'd help her get them back. Elba clutched her stomach as a wave of nausea rolled through her.

She sank down on the bed, and rested her head between knees, trying to breathe deep. Glancing at her watch, she decided it was time to check the room next door again to see if Hem was back. Before she could stand, a loud knock sounded on the door and she froze. Could it be the bureau? No one knew they were there.

"El? It's me."

At the sound of Kip's voice, Elba fell towards the door, wrenching it open. She looked over him, checking for signs of injury before taking a step back into the room, sagging with relief.

Kip paled at the sight of her fraught expression. Stepping into the room, he dropped the gym bag he was holding on the floor, closing the door behind him.

"Hey," he said. "Are you okay?"

Elba stared at the bag he'd dropped on the floor. It was hers. "Is that mine?" she asked.

Kip frowned, looking between her and the bag. "Yeah. I went and grabbed your stuff. What's wrong?"

"What's wrong?" Elba repeated. "You left! You just vanished."

He took a step towards her, his palms up. "I knew you'd be safe here for a few minutes. No one knows we're here."

"I wasn't worried about me." She shook her head, her hands trembling at her side. "What if they'd been waiting for you? What if they'd caught you?"

Kip sighed and took a step towards her. "I'm sorry. I should have given you more warning, but we need to move fast. The wards haven't been breached, but it's only a matter of time."

"It's not worth risking your life for some clothes," Elba bit out, taking a step back. She wasn't sure if she wanted to hug him or hit him. "Clothes can be replaced. You can't."

Kip's shoulders sagged. "I know. Maybe I shouldn't have bothered with your stuff, but I wanted you to be comfortable."

"Is Hem back?"

Kip glanced at the wall as though he could see him. "Yeah. I heard him banging about in his room when I was waiting for you to open the door."

Elba tried to take in a breath. They were all there and safe. "At least you're not in a suit," she joked. "I can go buy you some new stuff in the morning."

Kip looked away, taking a small step backwards. "I'm sorry," he said. "I'll be quick. Okay?"

"No." Elba gasped, eyes wide, as flames began to lick at his skin. There was no way he was going to throw himself into danger again. Before she could question herself, she dived forward and grabbed hold of his arm.

When the ground fell away beneath her, she fought against the screaming wind to hold on. Her grip started to slip as his sweater stretched against her weight and she cried out. What would happen if she lost her hold? Would she return to the hotel room or be lost in time and space forever? Panic and regret coursed through her as she clenched her fist tight around the material.

"What the fuck, Elba!"

She collapsed to the floor, trembling as they materialised in an unfamiliar bedroom. "I'm sorry," she wheezed.

"Do you have any idea how dangerous that was?"

Elba looked up at him, her eyes widening as she saw the terrified expression on his face.

"If you'd lost your grip . . ." He dragged a hand through his hair.

"I'm sorry," she whispered.

Kip sank to his knees beside her and gathered her to his chest. "It's okay. Just please, never do that again. You almost gave me a heart attack."

Elba closed her eyes, inhaling his warmth as her breathing began to even out. Part of her wanted to ask what would have happened if she'd lost her grip, but she decided against it. Some things were better off unknown.

"Come on," he said, rubbing her back and pressing a kiss to her head. "We need to get out of here."

Elba let him pull her to her feet, looking around for the first time. "Is this your apartment?" she asked.

"Yeah." He looked around the room with a frown. "Weird to think this will probably be the only time you get to see it."

Elba turned a slow circle, taking in the bedroom she'd wondered about so many times. She was bitterly disappointed. It had as much personality as his office. Decked out in whites, greys and pale pine, it had a distinctly clean and Scandinavian feel. She stepped to the door and peered out into the living room. It was the exact same layout as Hem's apartment the floor below, with the same minimalist feeling throughout. She frowned. Where was his stuff? Where was his personality? Even the art was geometric and monochrome. It was like a hotel.

"You can help if you want," Kip said from behind her.

Elba turned to find he'd thrown a large bag onto the bed and opened the wardrobe. "Sure," she said. "What do you want me to do?"

He nodded toward the open wardrobe. "Shove a few sweaters, shirts and pants in for me. I'll grab my toiletries."

Elba watched him disappear into the en suite, before turning to the painfully organised wardrobe. It was so functional. Everything hung neatly or folded precisely. Maybe he had a maid.

With a sigh, she stared pulling things off hangers and off shelves and packing them in the bag. She pulled open drawers, selecting socks and underwear to pack but when she opened the last drawer, she stopped.

Empty of clothes, the bottom drawer held an old biscuit tin. It shouldn't have seemed out of place, but it was the only thing she'd seen with any sort of personality and her fingers itched to see what was inside.

"You can pack that," Kip said softly behind her.

Elba jumped, pressing her hand to her chest. "Bloody hell, Kip. Don't sneak up on someone on the run."

He chuckled and reached around her to pull the tin from the drawer.

"What is it?" she asked as he carried it over to the bed.

Kip paused, his eyes on the tin, and Elba knew he was deciding whether or not to tell her.

She stepped closer. "It's okay. You don't have to tell me."

He frowned and shook his head. "No. I think I want to."

Elba tried to keep the excitement from her face as he sat down on the bed and placed the tin on his lap. She sat down beside him, curiosity itching beneath her skin as he pried off the lid, and she leaned against his arm as he tipped the open tin towards her. It was filled with photos, postcards and trinkets. He flipped over a few things and she spotted a trading card, a cartoon ripped from a newspaper and a battered friendship bracelet.

"It's your memory box," she said.

He nodded. "It's the only stuff I have from before the bureau."

Elba's chest constricted. This tin was filled with the keepsakes of a twelve-year-old boy. The memories of a life stolen. She reached out and plucked up a faded photograph. Even though they were almost two decades younger, she recognised Marco and Iseppa—Kipling's parents. They were standing in front of what looked like an orchard, perhaps in Italy. It was the boy between them that drew Elba's attention, though. He looked just like a younger version of Kip, but his skin was tanned dark and his eyes were brown. He looked like Swift, but it couldn't be. Could it?

"It's me," Kip said, reading her thoughts.

She dragged her gaze from the photo. "How?"

Frowning, he took the photo from her, staring at it as though trying to solve a puzzle hidden within its worn and faded edges. "This was taken on holiday about a month before the bureau came and took me."

Elba reached over and squeezed his thigh. "What happened?"

His frown deepened, his eyes clouding with sadness as he placed the photo back in the tin, pressing the lid back down.

She opened her mouth to tell him it was okay—that he didn't have to talk about it—when Kip drew a shaky breath and continued.

"I got angry." He shook his head. "It was over nothing. They wanted me to come inside for dinner, but I was trying to fix the broken chain on my bike. I needed to fix it because I was going out with my friends afterwards and I knew they wouldn't wait for me. My mum asked me to come in for the tenth time and I snapped at her that I wasn't hungry."

Elba watched as he clenched his hands into fists on his lap, the pain of what happened all those years ago still etched on his face. She placed a hand over the nearest fist, stroking his fingers with hers.

"My dad came out and had a go at me for being disre-spectful. I could feel it—my magic—even though I didn't know what it was. It bubbled under my skin, stretching like air in a balloon, trying to get out. We got into a shouting match. I can't even remember half of what I said. I felt like I was burning from the inside out. And then I wasn't.

"I remember screaming. I'm still not sure whether it was me, my parents or both. I know I was on fire. I could see it in the reflection on the window. I was burning. I'd never been so scared in my life. Even though it didn't hurt like fire, it stretched and tore at me until I thought it was going to pull every last drop of breath from my lungs." He took a shud-dering breath, his eyes fixed on his hands. "One minute my mum was on her knees crying and my dad was calling an ambulance, the next, I was in hospital. Of course, there were no burns. I was fine. The only sign that anything had happened was that my skin was pale, and my eyes had turned silver. When I first woke up, my parents crossed them-selves. The fear in their eyes . . ." He shook his head.

Elba's chest ached, tears welling in her eyes as she pictured a frightened twelve-year-old Kipling. "It must have been terrifying."

He nodded. "It was. I was discharged the next day because they couldn't find anything wrong with me, but my parents couldn't look at me. Whenever I tried to hug them, they'd find a way to avoid it. Two days later, there was a knock at the door."

"The bureau," Elba breathed.

"I listened at my bedroom door as they told them that they'd heard about me and they had a special school they could take me to. It went quiet shortly after that and I couldn't hear a thing. Now, of course, I realise they must have cast a spell to contain their conversation. They took me with them that afternoon."

They sat in silence for a moment before Kip sighed and squeezed her hand. "So that's it. My big sad story."

Elba opened her mouth to reply, but the words stuck in her throat, a tear streaking down her cheek.

"Oh," he said, his eyes wide in surprise as he looked at her for the first time. "I didn't mean to make you cry."

She shook her head. "You shouldn't have had to go through that."

Kip shrugged, wiping the tear from her face. "It happens all the time. I wasn't the first and I won't be the last."

"That doesn't make it right," Elba said. "I'm so sorry it happened to you."

Before he could respond, she stood and moved between his legs, framing his face with her hands. "I hate that it happened to you. I hate that you have to carry that pain with you."

Kip turned his face, kissing her palm. "I try to focus on the good things, although some days it's easier than others. If it hadn't happened, I wouldn't have met Hem." He lifted his eyes to hers, reaching out to stroke her cheek. "I wouldn't have met you."

Elba closed the distance between them and kissed him, if only to stop more tears from falling. He wrapped his arms around her, his hands stroking her back as she lost her fingers in his dark curls.

It took her a second longer than it should have to register the loud bang from the living room as the door was kicked in. She jumped back, Kip's silver eyes wide with terror as he grabbed her arm, summoning the silver flames that would take them to safety.

"Stop!"

Elba turned to see two men in jeans and hoodies standing in the bedroom doorway, sparks and mist shooting from their outstretched hands. The ground that had started to disappear beneath her feet solidified again as a burst of green mist struck Kip's shoulder sending him sprawling back onto the bed and out of her grip.

Elba stepped backwards, blood roaring in her ears as she looked between Kip, sitting back up with a groan, and the two men advancing towards them. The one with green mist encircling his fists sent another burst out at Kip, but this time he deflected it with a rush of silver flames, followed by a right hook and a kick to the chest that sent the blond-haired man flying backwards into the wardrobe, cracking the wooden slats.

Before Elba could summon the flames licking at her fingertips, the brown-haired man was on her. He grabbed her, pulling her to his chest, red sparks crackling at the fingertips he held to her neck.

"Stand down, Kipling," he barked at her ear. "Stand down or I'll melt your girlfriend's pretty face."

Rage unlike anything Elba had ever seen flickered across Kip's face. "Don't you lay a fucking finger on her, Bennet," he snarled.

The blond stood, dusting himself off. "You're not in a position to bargain, traitor."

Kip glared at him, flames still licking at his tensed fingers as he searched for a way out of the situation. "You haven't got a clue what you're talking about, Jay."

"Oh, don't we?" Jay sneered. "We know you helped a piece of Freedom scum escape. We know you've turned your back on us."

"Count yourself lucky Pearson wants you brought in alive," Bennet said. "Or you'd both be dead right now."

One of his red sparks jumped, settling on her skin where it burned like an ember from a fire, causing her to yelp.

Kip's magic flared, enveloping his forearms as he stepped toward her, but Bennet pulled her back.

"Where's the conduit stone, Kipling?"

Elba's heart skipped a beat as a new voice sounded from the doorway. A grey-haired man in a suit stood, arms folded, as he surveyed the scene, a brown-haired woman at his side, orange flames readied in her hands.

"I don't know what you're talking about," Kip spat.

The man raised a dark eyebrow. "Well, that I don't believe."

Elba watched, frozen, as he mumbled a spell under his breath, calling forward a small blue orb of light. Glancing at Kip in question, she found him staring, his jaw clenched. Whatever the orb was, it wasn't good.

Not daring to breathe as the orb made its way across the room, she realised too late that it was heading to her. To her chest.

"Funny that," the grey-haired man said, giving Jay a nod.

As the blond man strode over to her, Elba tried to back away, but Bennet held her in place. She kicked out in desperation, but he tightened his grip around her neck, the sparks sizzling against her skin until she cried out.

"Don't you fucking touch her!" Kip yelled, pushing between them.

The woman sent strings of orange flame shooting forward, twining around Kip, pinning his arms to his side. Elba watched, open mouthed, as Jay reached forward and shoved his hand down her sweater, fishing the stone from her bra.

"What's this, then?" he asked, holding the stone up.

The grey-haired man stepped forward and took the stone, turning it over in his hands. "Why would you lie to us, Kipling? I thought we were friends?"

"Is this how you treat friends, Karl?" Kip scoffed.

Elba tried to take a breath, despite the sharp pain of the burns against her neck and cheeks. They were outnumbered. They were going to get taken back to the bureau and it was her fault. If she hadn't grabbed hold of him, he would have packed his bag and been back at the hotel in minutes.

Her heart heavy and her eyes burning with tears, Elba turned to look at Kip. There was no defeat in his eyes, though. Instead, he watched as Jay and Karl inspected the stone, his face a picture of calm.

As if sensing her attention, he glanced at her, giving her the smallest of reassuring smiles. Elba frowned. He hadn't tried to convince them that the bureau was hiding things from them. He hadn't told them about the restrictors. Elba swallowed her gasp as realisation hit her. Kipling was stronger than they knew. But even if he could take out two of them, there were two more. They were still outnumbered. If only she'd used her magic sooner. Now, with the conduit stone gone, she was helpless.

Even as the thought formed in her mind, she felt it—the invisible string connecting her and Kip. It was still there. She frowned. Beneath her skin, the magic flickered and sparked, ready to be commanded. How was it possible?

When Kip looked at her again, she raised her eyebrows. Had he felt the connection still there? Had he known? He gave her an almost imperceptible nod as the flames at his fingertips started to swell.

Panic swirled in her gut. What did Kip expect her to do? She might end up burning the place to the ground. Then again, maybe that's exactly what he wanted. She pulled at the power surging inside her, ready to do whatever she could to break free of them long enough that Kip could magic them away to the hotel, where hopefully they wouldn't be able to follow.

A plume of black smoke exploded in the centre of the room and Elba yelped as Hem materialised between them. He sent a blast of power out, knocking a shocked Karl to the wall as he threw a punch at Jay. With a roar, Kip burst free of the woman's restraints, blasting her with his flames. Elba felt Bennet's arm tense around her neck and, closing her eyes, she commanded the flames to rip from her back and arms. He screamed as he let go, flailing backwards into the bathroom door, his clothes alight.

Elba turned back to the others to find Kip delivering a knockout punch to Karl as Hem knocked the woman out with a blast of black smoke. Spinning around, Kip snatched hold of her hand, silver flames swallowing them whole as they left his apartment behind.

FOURTEEN

KIP DROPPED the bag she hadn't even noticed he'd grabbed and took her face in his hands, his eyes wide. "Are you okay?" he asked, his breath ragged. "Did he hurt you?"

Elba opened her mouth to assure him that she was fine, but he gripped her chin gently, turning her head as he swore under his breath.

"What is it?" Hem asked, coming to stand beside him.

Calling forth his magic, Kip's face fell into a frown. "The bastard burned her with those fucking sparks."

Elba winced as the magic soothed the stinging sensation on her skin. Masked by adrenaline, she hadn't realised quite how sore it was.

Kip's hands slid to her shoulders as he resumed his inspection. Reaching out, she took his face in her hands, forcing him to look at her.

"I'm fine," she said as his eyes focused on her at last. "I'm fine."

He exhaled and pulled her to his chest, wrapping his arms around her.

"How did you know we were in trouble?" Elba asked Hem.

He leaned against the dressing table, holding up his hand to show the linking ring, before folding his arms. "I knew Kip was in trouble and put two and two together."

"I'm sorry," Elba moaned, burying her face in Kip's sweater. "I'm so sorry."

Kip didn't release his hold as he stroked her hair. "What are you apologising for?"

"It's my fault." She closed her eyes and drew a shaky breath. "If I hadn't been there . . . I made you stay longer. You wouldn't have been there—"

"Shh," Kip hushed her. "We're all okay. Going back to the apartments was always a risk."

"They got the stone, though." Elba shuddered at the memory of Jay's hand groping inside her sweater.

"What?" Hem said. "They got the conduit stone?"

Elba felt Kip nod his head from where he rested his chin on her hair. "Bastards."

"But how did Elba use magic, then?" Hem asked.

Elba stepped out from Kip's arms, his touch lingering until the last possible second. Noting the scorch marks with a shudder, she pulled down the front of her sweater, to show the faint blue glowing lines of the conduit stone scar, half concealed by her bra.

"Shit," Hem breathed. "That's not normal."

Elba raised an eyebrow and covered herself again. "I can't remember what normal is anymore."

"So, does that mean you and Kip are linked forever now?" Hem asked, looking between the two of them.

"You know as much as we do," Kip said, giving him a warning look.

Elba perched on the bed, her mind reeling. "You knew them all, didn't you? The Men."

"Yeah," Kip said, sitting beside her and taking her hand in his. "To be fair, Bennet has always been a prick."

"What about that older guy?" she asked.

Hem pulled a slatted chair from the dressing table and slumped in it. "What? Karl? He's like—"

"A supervisor," Kip finished. "We have units and he's the head of our unit."

Hem snorted. "I think after today we're fired."

Elba pressed her fingers to her temples, trying to organise the pieces of the puzzle. "Who's that Pearson person he mentioned then?"

Both Hem and Kip stiffened, and she raised her eyebrows.

"Pearson is the top of the food chain," Hem explained. "The boss."

Elba looked between the two men, trying to read the tension on their faces. "I thought the Grand Wizard was the top."

Kip shook his head. "The GW is the top. He's the very top. Like, for the world. Think of the bureau like a multinational company. The GW is the billionaire owner that the people working for the company never ever see. Pearson is the head of the British office. He and the heads from the other countries get together and decide on most of the rules. They're the only ones who get to meet with or even see the GW."

"The fact that Pearson himself put out an order to bring us in is terrifying," Hem said, his voice tight. "We must be on the most wanted list."

Silence fell over them as Elba tried to digest what they'd said. They knew they'd be in big trouble when they rescued Selena, but had they really thought about every Man in the country looking for them?

"How did they know about the conduit stone?" Hem asked, breaking the silence.

Kip exhaled, leaning forward and resting his forearms on his knees. "I have no idea. I mean, they knew we were trying to bring in an artefact the night we met Elba, but even we didn't know it was a conduit stone at that point."

"Could Selena have told them?" Elba asked.

Hem shook his head. "You saw her in that interrogation. She didn't say a word. Unless they dragged her in again between then and us breaking her out . . ."

Every question seemed to result in ten more and exhaustion weighed heavy on them all.

"This has officially been the longest day in history," Hem said, slapping his hands on his thighs before standing. "I am going to take a shower, order some food and fall asleep watching the shittiest program I can find. See you kids in the morning."

Elba managed a smile as he disappeared in a plume of black smoke. "That's just lazy," she said. "I mean, the door is right there."

"Old habits." Kip chuckled before turning his gaze to the bags abandoned on the floor. "Shall we unpack in the morning? I don't think I can face it."

"Why was your apartment so plain?" The question fell from her lips before she could stop it and her cheeks heated as Kip stared at her, his eyebrows raised.

"Excuse me?" he said, the corners of his mouth twitching.

Elba swallowed. "I'm sorry. That's not what I meant."

"What did you mean, then?"

She groaned and pinched the bridge of her nose. "I mean, where's your stuff? I expected your apartment to be more like Hem's office."

Kip's smile faded, his eyes shuttering. "Are you hungry? What do you want to eat?"

"I'm sorry," she said. "I shouldn't have asked."

Kip frowned, his eyes focused on her chest. "Are you okay?"

Following his gaze, she realised she was stroking her scar. She blinked in surprise. "Yeah. I'm fine. I guess it tickles a little bit. I didn't even notice I was touching it."

"Can I have a proper look?" Kip asked.

Elba grinned. "If you want me to get undressed, you don't have to make excuses."

Her comment didn't remove the frown from Kip's face and her heart rate accelerated. How worried was he that she was still connected to his magic? She pulled the sweater off over her head, shivering as he reached out and traced a finger over the glowing lines.

"How does it feel to you?" he asked, his eyes fixed on the swirling pattern.

"The scar?"

He raised his eyes to meet hers. "No, the link between us."

"Like a thin silver rope," she said. "Just beneath my ribs."

Kip nodded thoughtfully as though agreeing. "I need to teach you to control the magic properly."

Excitement flickered in her chest. "Really?"

"We have no idea how long this is going to last. The amount of power you can call on could be devastating if used incorrectly."

"So, like spells and stuff?" she asked.

"We can do spells, but just wielding first. I don't want you incinerating the hotel by accident." A hint of laughter sparked in his eyes and Elba felt herself relax just a little.

"Teach me," she said.

He raised his eyebrows. "What? Now?"

"Why not? The bureau could appear at any time, right? I managed to fend off that Bennet guy but only really because we had the element of surprise. They weren't expecting you and Hem to be so powerful and they thought they'd cut off my power."

Kip pressed his lips together, his eyes narrowed. "Fine."

Fighting the urge to squeal with excitement, Elba forced her expression into something she hoped was serious.

"I imagine water," Kip said. "I'm assuming that if you do the same, it will work the same as it's my borrowed power. I mean, I've never taught anyone before, so—"

"Water?" Elba interrupted. "To control flames?"

"If I want the flames to be harmless, I imagine water," he explained. "If I want them to burn, then I imagine fire."

Elba stared at her hands, summoning the silver flames. "How come it doesn't burn us?"

"I have no idea," Kip shrugged. "It just doesn't."

She thought of twelve-year old Kip, burning in his garden and her stomach flipped. Shaking the image from her mind, she looked around the bare hotel room for inspiration.

"Use me," Kip said, getting to his feet. "You can't burn me with my own magic, so I'm probably the safest option."

Elba baulked as he sat down in the wooden chair Hem had pulled from the table. "What if I set fire to the chair?"

He raised an eyebrow. "Don't."

"Helpful."

Shaking her hands out to her sides, she imagined streams of flowing water and commanded the power to reach out and wrap around Kip the same way she'd practiced with Hem's smoke before the warehouse. A burst of flame licked out towards him but flickered out before it could form anything that resembled a rope.

"Try again," Kip said, smiling at the disappointment on her face.

Taking a deep breath, Elba held out her hands and imagined watery ropes wrapping around Kip's middle, tying him to the chair. This time, the magic held long enough to loop around him before evaporating into nothingness.

"You're getting there," he said, giving her an encouraging smile. "Think of water but give it a quality. For example, if you want it to be strong, think of steel or something similar."

"Metal water." Elba pulled a face. "Sure."

Kip rolled his eyes. "Give me a break. It's the first time I've had to explain how I control my magic, and it's very distracting when my student is in her bra."

Elba glanced down in surprise. "Oh. Sorry. I'll put my sweater back on—"

"Don't."

Elba's stomach clenched at his tone. She met his gaze, her heart racing at the intent in his silver eyes. Summoning the flames again, she pictured watery steel ropes sliding out towards Kip. This time, she aimed them at his ankles, binding them to the legs of the chair. They formed and held.

"It worked!" She squealed.

Kip leant forward, inspecting the flaming cuffs around his ankles. "Impressive. They should stay there as long as you will them to. To make them disappear, just command them to fade."

Elba's heart pounded in her chest as Kip looked up at her questioningly. "Put your hands behind your back," she said.

"Excuse me?"

"I want to practise more," she said, swallowing.

Kip narrowed his eyes but slowly clasped his hands together behind the chair. Before she could think better of it, she sent flaming cuffs out, encircling his wrists, binding him to the chair.

"What now?" Kip asked, realisation flashing in his eyes.

Elba stepped between his spread legs and fisted his hair, tipping his head back as she claimed his mouth. The deep moan that reverberated from Kip's chest sent a jolt through her core and she kissed him harder, her tongue fighting for dominance until she stepped back, breathless.

Holding his gaze, Elba reached behind her back and unfastened her bra, her nipples hardening in the cool air. She could tell he was trying to keep his eyes on hers, but his gaze dropped to her breasts, his pupils darkening as he licked his lips.

Elba tried to calm her trembling fingers as she unfastened her jeans, shimmying out of them, underwear and all, until she was naked in front of him.

"Elba," he ground out, the word almost unrecognisable.

She stepped forward again, and he strained against the flaming cuffs, but she commanded them to stay strong. "Try and break out of them again and I'll tighten them," she whispered against his lips.

He tried to catch her mouth with his, but she gripped his hair again, pulling his head back until he was looking at the ceiling. She held him there as she leant forward and dragged her tongue along the column of his neck, over his Adam's apple. He groaned and she let go, stepping back again.

Elba dropped to her knees between his legs and, holding his gaze, she unfastened his jeans. He lifted his hips just enough for her to pull both his jeans and boxers down to his knees and she smiled as she took in his hard, straining length.

"Make them disappear," she whispered.

Kip held her gaze, his breathing heavy as he uttered the words that vanished his clothes.

Leaning forward, she stuck out her tongue and slowly licked the length of his shaft. Kip inhaled sharply and she allowed herself a small grin before running her tongue across the sensitive head, causing it to twitch.

"Elba," Kip growled in warning.

She slid her mouth over him, taking him as deep as she could. He swore loudly and the groan she coaxed from him as she worked him with her tongue caused heat to pool between her legs in an almost painful ache. She slid him in and out of her mouth, caressing him with her tongue, allowing his moans and ragged breathing to light every nerve in her tingling body on fire.

Pulling back with a final flick of her tongue, she stood, taking in the look of awe on Kip's beautiful face. As he took in the sight of her standing in front of him, his eyes flashed, the serene look morphing into something so animalistic, it stole Elba's breath.

"Let me go," he growled.

Elba shook her head.

He frowned, his jaw set. "Elba."

When he struggled against the restraints, Elba tutted and commanded them tighter. Kip hissed, swearing under his breath. She stared at the way the muscles in his shoulders curved, the deep line between his pectorals, splicing between his abs. His muscles flexed as he tugged against the restraints and she swallowed, revelling in the fact that this gorgeous god of a man was hers. And she currently had him rock hard and tied to a chair.

Her body trembling with need, Elba straddled his lap, balancing on her tiptoes as she took his hard length in her hand.

"You're going to be the death of me, Elba." Kip groaned, tipping his head back as she stroked him.

Guiding him inside her, she couldn't contain her sigh of pleasure as he filled her. Kip's moan set fire to her insides and she placed her hands on his shoulders to steady herself as she slowly rode him, savouring every shuddering burst of pleasure.

"Elba," he pleaded, trying to capture her mouth, her neck, her breasts with his mouth, but she kept him at arm's length.

She ground against him, a breathless moan escaping her lips as she felt her pleasure building.

"Elba," he repeated. "Please."

She paused, her entire body throbbing. "Are you begging, Kipling?"

He narrowed his eyes, a tight smile on his perfect lips. "Yes."

She held his silver gaze as she began to move again, undulating her hips as the pleasure continued to build.

"You want to play dirty?" Kip ground out. "Fine."

Before she could ask what he meant, licks of flame crept over her body, teasing her nipples and racing up and down her skin. She cried out in surprise, the sensation too much to

114

bear as it tipped her over the edge, her orgasm shuddering through her.

Perhaps Kip had known that she would lose concentration as her vision darkened at the edges, her body trembling, and before she knew what was happening, his restraints had vanished and he was lifting her up, throwing her on the bed.

Elba threw back her head, arching as he kissed and touched every available inch of her skin as though he might never get the chance again. His name tore from her throat as he sucked her nipple into his mouth, his hand massaging her other breast. Kip claimed her lips as he thrust into her and she dug her nails into his back, wrapping her legs around his waist. Holding himself over her, his other hand gripped her buttock so tightly she yelped, as he slammed into her again and again.

Elba clung to him, moaning his name as her pleasure built once more. This time, she felt silver flames flicker across her skin as she clenched around him, her cry of ecstasy filling the room. Kip clutched her to him as he shuddered through his own release, moaning her name against her neck.

Once their breathing had levelled, Kip pushed up to look at her. "Fucking hell, Elba."

She felt her cheeks heat. "Too much?"

He laughed, the vibrations sending ghosts of pleasure from where he was still inside her. "No. Not too much. Never too much. That was epic."

She smiled and he bent down to kiss her before untangling himself and lying down beside her. He pulled her to his chest, his heart still pounding.

"Looks like you're a better teacher than you thought," Elba said, trailing her fingers up and down his chest.

He kissed the tip of her nose. "Despite the distractions."

Elba laughed, but when she looked up at his face, she noted his smile had faded into the serious expression she'd become so accustomed to.

"What?" she asked, stroking his cheek.

He turned to look at her, his eyes taking in every inch of her face before returning her gaze. "I guess I don't bother buying anything that I like, because I know I won't be able to keep it."

Elba frowned, realising he was talking about his apartment. "Why wouldn't you be able to keep it?"

He raised his eyebrows, and she bit her lip. He'd likely never set foot in that apartment again. If it had been filled with mementos and furniture he loved, it would all be gone now. "You didn't know that was going to happen, though," she pushed. "How long did you live there?"

"Years."

Elba watched him carefully. "So, you didn't allow yourself anything you liked on the off chance this would happen?"

"It's not the off chance," he said, his gaze drifting from hers. "I've never been able to keep anything. Nothing lasts."

Elba's heart wrenched at the sadness in his eyes. Reaching out, she ran a hand through his hair, trailing her fingers down his cheek until he looked at her again. "It's time to stop thinking like that," she whispered. "Because you get to keep me."

Kip shook his head, his gaze slipping again, but she pushed up onto her elbow, taking his face in her hands.

"You get to keep me," she repeated, punctuating her words with a kiss.

Sadness glistened in his eyes, but she pressed kiss after kiss to his lips until it faded.

"Say it again," he whispered, leaning his forehead against hers.

Elba smiled, kissing the tip of his nose. "You get to keep me."

FIFTEEN

ELBA WOKE to Kip's warm breath against her neck, his arm tucking her against him. She smiled into her pillow wondering if there was a better way to wake up. Turning her head to look at him, he loosed a quiet groan, pressing a kiss to her shoulder.

"Good morning." Elba grinned, savouring the feel of his warm, naked body pressed around hers.

He held her tighter, causing her to gasp at the feel of his hardness against her back. "Morning," he rumbled.

Their magic lessons had carried on way into the night—the practical and defensive interspersed with exploration of pleasure. She trembled at the memory.

"Did you sleep well?" she asked.

In answer, Kip trailed soft kisses down her arm, guiding her onto her back as he swept his tongue over her nipple. Elba sucked in a breath, arching into his touch as he shifted to pay her other breast equal attention. The kisses moved down her stomach and she fisted the bedcovers as Kip's head dipped, running his tongue slowly between her legs, circling her clit. The moan that shuddered through her was interrupted by a loud knock at the door.

"You two had better be awake," Hem called.

Elba pushed up onto her elbows as Kip groaned his annoyance against her. The vibrations caused her to tense, and he smiled, spreading her wider as he returned to tasting her.

"I'm only knocking as a warning," Hem continued. "I've brought coffee."

"Kip," Elba breathed. "We should—"

He lifted his head and glared at the door. "Fuck off, Hem!"

"Thirty seconds!" Hem shouted. "I don't care if you're naked."

Kip crawled back up the bed, collapsing face down beside her. "I fucking hate him."

Elba chuckled, moving to slide out of bed towards her unpacked bag of clothes. "No, you don't."

"I'll make up for that interruption later," Kip said, stopping her with a hand on her waist. "That's a promise."

The soft intensity of his words sent a jolt through her core and she looked away, her cheeks heating.

Elba had barely finished pulling her sweats on when Hemingway materialised in a cloud of black smoke, a tray of coffees in his hands.

"There we go," he said, smiling at Elba as he held out a coffee. "Wasn't so hard, was it?"

She gave him a withering look and took the coffee. "I think the coffee would still have been hot after five minutes."

Hem raised an eyebrow at Kip, who was still in bed, half under the covers. "Five minutes? Losing your stamina in your old age?"

"No. I'm just *that* good, mate." He threw back the covers and strode towards him, completely naked and still hard.

"For fucksake, Kip!" Hem barked, closing his eyes and turning away. "Why? *Why?*"

Elba watched, lips pressed together as Kip took a coffee

from the tray and winked at her. "You were so eager to barge in here, I thought it's what you wanted?"

Hem muttered a string of obscenities under his breath and turned to face Elba, ignoring Kip as he fished in his bag for clothes.

"How are you feeling this morning?" he asked.

She knew he wasn't talking about how she'd slept. "Okay. Considering the magical world is out to get us."

"That's what we need to talk about," Hem said, pulling the small square of paper from his pocket.

Kip sank down onto the edge of the bed, grey sweats slung low on his hips. "Did you write to him already?"

"Yeah. Just before I picked up the coffees. I told him we want our answers as promised."

Elba cradled the corrugated paper cup between her hands. The Freedoms had torn down Kipling and Hemingway's entire world. Would what Lawrence tell them make it all worth it? What if it wasn't? Was there anywhere they could run to? Hide?

"Wait a second," Hem said, holding up the paper. "We've got mail."

He placed the small square on the dressing table so they could all sit it.

Slater's Museum of Modern Art. 9am.

"9am?" Kip said. "What time is it now?"

Hem looked at his watch. "Quarter to eight."

"Are you kidding me?" Kip asked, grabbing Hem's wrist to check for himself. "Why the fuck are you waking us up so early?"

"We're wanted criminals," Hem snapped. "We have shit to do. You can't spend all day shagging."

Elba flinched.

"I'm sorry." He shook his head. "I'm just stressed and tired. I didn't think noise cancelling headphones were a necessity when I packed my bag, so I didn't get much sleep."

He looked pointedly at Kip who had the decency to look a little bashful.

"Sorry," Elba said, her cheeks burning as her mind flipped through the dozens of times she'd cried out Kip's name during the night. It was a marvel they'd not had someone bang on the wall or door.

Hem flashed her a smile as he snatched up the magical paper and shoved it back in his pocket. "It's fine. Just get Kip to cast a muffler spell next time or something. I'm going to go see if I can sweet talk whoever's on reception into letting me use their internet. I'll find out where this Slater place is and figure out where we can magic to."

"Good idea," Kip said, draining his coffee. "I don't want to be out in the open for any longer than we have to be."

"Let's plan on leaving in an hour," Hem said, moving to the door.

"Wait a minute," Elba said. "Can you see if there's somewhere near the museum we can get some breakfast? I'm starving."

Her stomach rumbled as if to punctuate the point and Hem laughed. "Sure. Can you be ready to go in twenty minutes?"

She grinned. "Definitely."

As Hem closed the door behind him, Kip stepped behind her, slipping his arms around her waist as he pressed a kiss to her neck. "I was a lot more excited about an hour," he murmured.

Elba laughed. "I don't think I have enough energy to last an hour."

"Twenty minutes it is then," he said.

She stepped out of his embrace, trying to give him what she hoped was a stern expression, but if the grin on his face was anything to go by, it wasn't working. "Aren't you tired?"

Kip stepped to her again, resting his hands on her hips. "Of you? Never."

She melted into his kiss as his fingers pulled her closer but forced herself to step back. "Stop it," she scolded. "I'm going to take a shower."

"Good idea," Kip said, dropping his sweats and stepping out of them.

Elba squawked in protest as he backed toward the shower. "Hey!"

"I'll wash your back if you wash mine," he offered, his eyes dancing with laughter.

Although she rolled her eyes as she followed after him, Elba's heart swelled at the light in his eyes. She wouldn't have thought it possible, but happiness made him even more gorgeous.

When he held out his hand to pull her into the tiny bathroom, she laughed and took it.

SIXTEEN

"ARE YOU GOING TO CHEW THAT?"

"I'm hungry." Hem shot Kipling a look before returning to his full English breakfast.

Elba smiled as she sipped her tea. Sitting in the museum's small café, it would almost be easy to forget that their lives were on the line.

"This isn't half bad," Kip said, eyeing his avocado toast.

Hem shook his head. "First of all, you'd have to be a really shit café to mess up spreading avocado mush on toast. Second of all, it's a museum of modern art."

Elba fought the twitching corners of her mouth. "What does that have to do with anything?"

"It means it's fancy."

Kip choked on his mouthful of toast and Elba smiled.

"You're adorable," she said.

"I know."

They sat in comfortable silence for a moment, the clinking of cutlery on plates the only sound until Hem chuckled to himself.

Kip glanced at Elba, before turning to Hem, eyebrows raised. "What's up, mate?"

Hem shook his head, still smiling. "I just realised some-thing. We're unemployed for the first time in our lives."

"Shit." Kip exhaled as he placed his coffee cup down.

Elba looked between the two of them, trying to imagine them working in a Normal office. Perhaps she could get them a job at the call centre . . . The smile faded from her lips.

"What's wrong?" Kip asked, placing his hand over hers. "You don't need to worry about us. We'll figure it out. We could always hire Hem out as a stripper or something."

Hem snorted but Elba just stared, her stomach churning around her muesli and yogurt.

"I haven't been to work in almost a week," she said. "I assume I'm sacked, too."

"Either that," Hem said, "or they've called the police."

Elba sat up, her heart dropping to her stomach. "Shit! Saba!"

"Do you have your phone with you?" Kip asked.

She shook her head. "No. It's switched off and on the bedside table."

"Be right back." He wiped his hands with a napkin and disappeared towards the toilets.

Elba watched him, her hand moving to her stomach as it roiled with nerves. "We can't use our phones, though," she said. "What if they track us?"

"There's a spell," Hem said around a mouthful of sausage. "It'll only give you five minutes, but you can call your office or Saba and let them know you're alive."

She looked towards the toilets in time to see Kip striding back over to them, her phone in his hand. Elba took it from him with a grateful smile.

"You realise it looks like you took your phone into the toilet, right?" Hem said.

Kip rolled his eyes and sank back into his chair, a faint glimmer of magic escaping his fingers as he warmed the remaining coffee in his cup. "Did Hem explain?" he asked.

Elba nodded. "Five minutes."

"Yeah. But try and keep it less than that." He pressed his fingers to the phone and muttered an incantation. "Okay, turn it on."

As the screen lit up, she tried to steady her breathing. What if Saba had called the police? Would they have gone to the apartment? What if they'd run into the bureau? Her phone began to ding incessantly, and she flicked it to silent.

Opening her messages, she pulled up Saba's thread, deciding to send her a voice note. If she called her, it would take a lot more than five minutes.

"Hey Saba. Sorry for being such a shit friend. Alex came back from Thailand and surprised me. It sent me on a bit of a spiral, so I've gone back to my parents' place for a bit. I'm handing my notice in today, too. Time for a fresh start. I'm having a bit of a phone detox, so my phone is going off again after this. I'll be in touch in a few days when I'm back. Hope you're okay." She pressed send and stared at her phone as the message sent.

"Handing in your notice?" Kip asked.

Elba took a deep breath, blowing it out slowly as she willed her hands to stop trembling. "Yes. There's nothing like almost dying to make you realise life is too short to be stuck in a dead-end job."

Kip smiled. "I think that's a great idea."

She opened her emails and sent an apology to her boss along with her formal resignation. Whatever the response was, it would have to wait as Hem tapped his watch. Elba's finger was reaching for the power off button when another string of messages caught her eye.

"Oh, shit! Shit! Shit!" She almost dropped the phone as she scrambled to open the thread, her eyes wide.

Kip and Hem both sat up, leaning over the table towards her.

"What's wrong?" Hem asked.

Elba looked up from her phone and swallowed. "My cousin. She's supposed to be staying with me. I completely forgot."

Kip and Hem breathed a collective sigh of relief and sat back in their seats.

"Well, that's okay," Kip said, reaching for his coffee again. "Just tell her she can't anymore."

Elba shook her head. "You don't understand. She's coming from Italy."

"A hotel?" Hem suggested.

"Whatever you're going to do, you've got thirty seconds to decide," Kip said, looking at his watch.

Elba stared at her phone in panic.

"When is she arriving?" Kip asked.

"She landed like twenty minutes ago," Elba said. "She was texting to confirm my address for the taxi."

"Tell her to go to the hotel," Kip suggested. "I'll magic back and ask the receptionist to give her a key to our room. Just make sure she understands she can't go to your apartment."

Elba nodded, typing out the text.

"Ten seconds," Hem said.

Elba gritted her teeth. "Not helping."

The message bleeped confirmation that it had sent, and she powered down the phone, chucking it onto the table as if it might explode.

Hem stared at it, lying dark amongst the empty plates. "Well, that was more stressful than I anticipated," Hem said.

Elba snorted. "You're telling me."

"Ten minutes until Lawrence shows," Kip said. "I'll go sort out the key."

Elba tried not to fidget as she waited both for him to return and for further information from Lawrence. They knew nothing more than what had appeared on the paper. Perhaps it would be Lawrence with his team as before, or maybe it would be someone else. The paper lay on the table amidst the empty packets of sugar and ketchup discarded by Hemingway and as Elba turned her attention to it, the writing faded—the letters turning into new ones.

"Look," she hissed, leaning forward to read it.

Barford exhibit.

Elba's stomach churned. "Does that mean they're here?"

"Either that, or they will be soon." Hem wiped his mouth with a napkin and tossed it on his plate, glancing over his shoulder to see Kip striding towards them. "Let's go. Anyone know where we're heading?"

"The sculpture hall," Kip said appearing at the table and shrugging on his leather jacket. "Barnaby Barford is a British sculptor."

Elba shared a surprised look with Hem. "I didn't know you were into art."

"You never asked," he replied with a wink.

Hem snorted. "Go on then. Who else do you like?"

"In this museum?" Kip raised an eyebrow at his tone. "I saw that Christy Lee Rogers has a few pieces on show that I'd love to see if we weren't risking our lives to meet with the enemy."

"Are they the enemy, though?" Elba asked as they moved through the artfully lit hallways.

Kip frowned, his eyes flitting along the artwork as they passed. "That all depends on what Lawrence has to say for himself."

The sculpture hall wasn't what Elba was expecting. She'd been to the Louvre once as a teenager and her idea of sculpture was tall white lifelike statues—usually nude. Her eyes widened as she took in the large tree in the centre of the room, a tangle of what looked like green wire with large red apples amongst the whorls. She couldn't stop herself from moving towards a large tiger constructed from what looked like small coloured discs but before she could take a closer look, footsteps broke through the silence of the large room.

Lawrence strode in, the same guards as before flanking him on either side. He didn't ask this time before summoning his magic. Elba felt the tingle as it settled around the room. She wondered what would happen if someone wanted to come in, but the stony faces of the Freedoms posted at the doorway would probably be enough to deter any unwanted attention.

"Good morning," Lawrence said, looking at each of them in turn. "Thank you."

"For what?" Hem said, eyeing his guards as he folded his arms across his chest. "Putting our asses on the line for possibly no reason whatsoever?"

Lawrence raised his eyebrows. "Even if you aren't satisfied with my answers—which I can assure you, you will be— you wanted to save Selena anyway."

"Oh, really?" Hem countered.

"Yes, Hemingway." A rueful smile curved his lips as Hem tensed. "I know all about you and Kipling."

Elba's heart slammed steadily against her ribs. She watched the guards warily, wondering whether they'd be able to magic out if needed.

"Don't be alarmed," Lawrence continued. "Selena told me all about you both. She was distraught when you decided not to join us."

Hem clenched his teeth but said nothing. Beside him, Kip shifted slightly toward him. Whether it was in solidarity or to hold him back, Elba wasn't sure.

Lawrence stepped closer. "I know I have a long way to go before you'll believe we're not the bad guys, but I'm hoping you'll allow me to offer our side of the story."

"I'm fairly certain that the 'good guys' don't kidnap people and carve them to pieces," Kip ground out.

Elba flinched, thinking of him strung up in the warehouse,

his body bleeding and battered. She cursed the fact that she was so far away from him, suddenly desperate to touch him —to comfort him.

"Naomi wasn't the best poster girl for us," Lawrence admitted, his face falling into a frown. "She had so much anger. We tried to rein her in, but her thirst for revenge was just too strong."

"Is it true, then?" Elba said, stepping forward. "Did the bureau murder her family?"

Lawrence's expression darkened further. "Yes. Naomi was one of our first recruits and her role was to reach into the bureau and try to spread word of what was happening."

"I don't remember Naomi," Kip said. "She worked at the bureau?"

Lawrence nodded. "She was First Tier."

At Hem's small intake of breath, Elba raised her eyebrows. "What does that mean?"

"That's upper management," Kip explained, his expression one of disbelief. "The same level as Pearson."

"What happened?" Elba pressed. The air in the sculpture hall seemed colder all of a sudden, and she wrapped her arms around herself.

Lawrence sighed and turned to examine the tree in the centre of the room. "I think to best explain things, I should start at the beginning."

Elba watched as he sank down onto a shiny white bench, clasping his hands together on his lap. He must only have been in his late twenties, but as he looked up at them, his weariness aged him a decade.

"Four years ago, the First Tier rose up in a coup against the Grand Wizard—"

"Bullshit," Hem interrupted.

Lawrence exhaled and shook his head. "That reaction is exactly why it's not public knowledge. Why we've found it so hard to spread the truth. It's exactly what Pearson and the rest of the First Tier planned on happening."

Kip pressed his fingers against his temple. "What did this coup entail?"

"They kidnapped the Grand Wizard," Lawrence explained, "with the intent of harnessing his power for themselves."

Hem laughed, shaking his head. "This is bollocks. If the GW had been kidnapped, we'd know about it."

"Would you, though?" Lawrence asked. "Have you ever even seen the Grand Wizard?"

Elba stared between Lawrence's pained expression and Kip and Hem, her brain aching with questions. "So how do the Freedoms tie into this?"

"There are no 'Freedoms'," Lawrence replied with a sniff. "The 'Freedoms' were created by the bureau to turn the Men against us."

"I can't believe you expect us to believe this," Kip said. "We've heard your people refer to themselves as 'Freedoms'."

Lawrence shook his head. "Some members tried to claim the name for themselves. They thought that as they were already called it, they might as well own it. The freedom wasn't about freedom of magic, though. It was about freedom for the Grand Wizard."

"So, the First Tier was plotting against the GW?" Hem asked. "How would they even be strong enough to take him down?"

Lawrence ran a hand through his short brown hair. "The Grand Wizard had grown complacent. In his position of power, he became more of a figure head, visiting different countries and checking in without actually making any decisions. The British Men of Magic realised this and had been in control of operations without running things by him for years. The restrictors for example. When the Grand Wizard found out about it, he was furious. He threatened to have the First Tier incarcerated."

"How did he find out?" Elba asked.

Lawrence gave her a sad smile. "Naomi. She had recently been promoted. The first promotion to the First Tier in fifteen years. They misjudged her ruthless nature and tenacity, thinking she would support them. They judged her wrong. Her loyalty was with the Grand Wizard until the day she died."

Elba shuddered, recalling the moment Naomi took her own life right in front of her. For the first time, a slither of pity snaked across Elba's heart. She'd definitely lost her way over the years, but the bureau had shaped her into the monster she'd become.

"You're saying the bureau fabricated a war between the Men and ... what would you call yourselves?" Kip asked, his dark eyebrow arched.

"That's just it." Lawrence laughed bitterly. "We've become the Freedoms they wanted us to be. Our desperation and self-defence has painted us as murderers."

Overwhelmed by the influx of information, Elba stepped forward and perched on the other end of the bench. "So, Naomi tried to stop the kidnapping of the Grand Wizard, but what about the rest of you? How did the Freedoms form?"

Lawrence gave her a small smile. "They're mostly because of me. It started with my closest confidants and then spread out via word of mouth until our numbers grew. Of course, the restrictors helped. If we could convince people to check, it was easier to sway them to the truth."

"Why you, though?" Elba pressed. "Were you and Naomi . . . ?"

"No, no." Lawrence baulked. "It's because the Grand Wizard is my grandfather."

Hem swore loudly and Elba watched as Kip dragged a hand across his face with a groan.

"Even if what you're saying is true, what are they hoping to do with him?" Kip asked.

"The conduit stones," Elba whispered. At the silence that fell around her, she looked up, finding Hem and Kip staring at her in surprise. "It's why they were making such a big fuss about them, right?"

Lawrence nodded. "Yes. They think if they can gather enough stones for each of them, they'll be able to syphon the Grand Wizard's power, draining him until they've shared it between themselves."

"Is he that powerful?" Elba asked, holding Lawrence's gaze.

"The Grand Wizard is the source of magic for the entire world," he explained. "There is nothing and no one more powerful than him. Even with his power split between all five members of the First Tier, it would make them a hundred times more powerful than anyone else."

"What's their end goal?" Hem asked, his voice strained. "Are they literally trying to take over the world?"

Lawrence pressed his lips together. "Yes. As ridiculous as it sounds. They hope that they can coerce the other bureaus of the world under their rule."

"I need to sit down," Hem muttered.

Lawrence curled a finger and an identical bench appeared behind him and Kip. Elba raised her eyebrows at the flippant show of power. She'd seen things conjured from nothing before, but the effortlessness was astounding. No spell had been muttered, no swirling mist appearing. Only the faintest sparkle around his fingertip. If his grandfather was the most powerful magician on the planet, she wondered just how powerful Lawrence was.

"So, the Freedoms trying to steal all the magical artefacts . . ." Kip asked, sitting down on the bench.

Lawrence nodded. "We were trying to keep them from the bureau."

"I'm really sorry," Elba said, forcing herself to meet Lawrence's inquiring gaze. "We lost our conduit stone. The bureau ambushed us and took it."

"That's unfortunate," Lawrence said, pinching the bridge of his nose.

"What will happen to your grandfather if they use them?" she asked.

Lawrence turned his head to look at her. "If it works, he'll die. It's never been done before, but the experts we have at our headquarters seem to think that it would also wipe out his line."

Elba's stomach flipped. "You'd die?"

"It's possible." He wiped his palms on his thighs and stood. "I need to go. I can't linger in one place too long. My magic is too traceable. I'm sure you understand."

Elba got to her feet too, moving to stand between Hemingway and Kipling.

"What now?" Hem asked.

Lawrence glanced at the men and woman guarding the room. "That's up to you."

Kip glanced at her before settling his gaze on Hem. "We need to talk."

"Understandable." Lawrence flicked a hand and Elba felt the tickle of magic as the spell he'd surrounded the room with dissipated. "You have the paper. If you want to join us, just let me know. We can keep you safe."

With a brief nod in their direction, he turned and left, the guards falling in around him.

"Well, shit." Hem exhaled.

SEVENTEEN

KIP KEPT hold of Elba's hand as they arrived in the shadows beside the hotel. With her phone off, she had no idea whether her cousin would be waiting in the room for her or not. They walked into the lobby in silence, Hem and Kip still processing everything Lawrence had told them.

The reception desk was empty as they walked through to the stairs. When they'd left that morning, the teenage girl from the night before had been replaced by a young man in his twenties, who'd winked at her, almost gaining him a black eye from Kipling.

Reaching the door to their hotel room, Elba's heart pounded with a mix of nerves and excitement. She hadn't seen her cousin in person for almost two years. Kip gave her a reassuring smile as she took a deep breath and opened the door.

Elba squealed, her hands flying to her mouth as she found her cousin on the bed, riding the young man from the front desk. Her hands cupping her own breasts, her head was thrown back, trailing long dark hair down her back as she moaned. The man noticed them first, his eyes widening in terror as he tried to sit up.

Elba didn't dare look at Kip and Hem as the latter coughed loudly, amusement clear in his voice.

As flustered as the receptionist was, her cousin didn't seem bothered at all. If anything, she behaved like it was perfectly normal to be fucking a total stranger in your cousin's bed at eleven o'clock on a Monday afternoon.

"Elba! *Mia cara cugina*!" she squealed, wrapping a blanket around herself and dismounting.

The young man pulled on his boxers, clutching for clothes on his way out of the room. Kip and Hem barely moved to make way for him, and Elba cringed as he squeezed between them, his face bright red.

Before she could say anything, her cousin folded her into an embrace. "It's been too long," she said, her accent thicker than Elba remembered. She stepped back and rearranging the blankets clutched to her chest. "I missed you."

Elba opened and closed her mouth a couple of times, unsure what to say as she took in her cousin. She was a little shorter than Elba, sharing the same curves, but as both her parents were Italian, her skin and hair were darker, her eyes a deep chocolate brown. Those differences aside, they'd been mistaken for sisters most of their lives.

"Who are these two?" she asked, stepping back and looking Hem and Kip up and down. "Your bodyguards?"

Elba grinned, remembering how bowled over she'd been the first time she saw them. "Siena, meet Kipling and Hemingway."

"Siena," Hem mused. "Is everyone in your family named after places in Italy?"

Siena arched a dark eyebrow. "Are all of Elba's friends named after overrated authors?"

"Touché," Hem said with a dip of his head.

Siena held his gaze for a moment, unsmiling, before turning back to Elba and clasping her hands in hers. "Why are we here and not your apartment? Why is your phone turned off? Is everything okay?"

Elba paled. "It's a long story. I—"

"Rats," Kip said. "Her apartment has rats, so she's staying here while they get rid of them."

Siena wrinkled her nose. "How horrible."

Elba blushed at the lie, dipping her head. "I'm sorry I didn't give you much warning. My phone won't stay on longer than a few minutes at a time and I have to be honest, I completely forgot you were coming."

Siena laughed. "No problem. I'll book a room here, too. I want to catch up."

"I took the liberty of booking you a room already," Kip said with a smile.

Elba looked up at him in surprise.

"Oh," Siena hitched the blankets higher. "*Grazie.* That's very kind of you. Let me know how much I owe you."

Kip waved it off. "Honestly, it's fine. This place isn't exactly the Ritz."

Siena stared at him, assessing, as she took in the hand he slipped into Elba's. "Ah, so you're Elba's boyfriend?"

Elba tensed but Kip squeezed her hand and smiled. "Yes."

Her chest shamefully filling with butterflies, Elba turned to her cousin. "How about we catch up once you're settled in your room?"

Siena's smile faded. "I'm afraid I need to go into the office as soon as possible. Are you getting your phone fixed so I can contact you?"

"Yes," Elba said, hoping it was a real possibility. "Just let me know when you're free."

Siena pulled her into another hug, pressing a kiss to her cheek. "I'll call housekeeping to change the sheets. Don't worry. It was a stressful flight, so I needed to let off a little steam."

Elba's cheeks heated at the brazen admission. "Erm. Sure. We'll go wait in Hem's room while you get dressed."

"Hem's room?" Siena asked, turning back to them.

"I'm just next door," he said with a wink.

Siena stared at him, unimpressed. "Does your apartment have rats too?"

Kip snorted, covering it with a cough. Hem opened his mouth to retort, but Elba grabbed hold of his sleeve and tugged him through the door.

"Well, she's an absolute delight," he huffed as he swiped his key card through the lock, letting them into the room.

Kip shoved him playfully as he walked past. "You're only annoyed because she wasn't drooling over you. Tell me, what was that like?"

Hem narrowed his eyes and closed the door. "What is she here for anyway? She said something about an office?"

Elba sat down on the bed. "She does something technical to do with computers. I'm not entirely sure. She's been transferred from the Italian office. That's all I know."

Hem huffed and pulled the square of magic paper from his pocket, dropping it on the dresser. It lifted a little as he walked past and collapsed face down on the bed.

Kip frowned at it. "Do you think he was telling the truth?"

"I mean, it makes sense," Hem mumbled into the pillow.

Kip turned to him. "You believe that Lawrence is the son of the GW?"

"Why would he lie?"

Elba reached out and took hold of Kip's hand, tugging him toward where she was perched on the edge of the bed. He sighed and slumped down next to her.

"It's a lot to take in," she said, folding his hand between hers, "but I agree. It makes an awful lot of sense."

"It explains the private plane," Hem said, sitting back against the pillows. "If he's the GW's grandson, he'll be rolling in it."

Elba turned to look at him. "Really?"

"Uh, yes." Hem laughed. "The GW is literally the most powerful person on the planet. His family has been since the dawn of magic. He's beyond a billionaire."

"So, is Lawrence next in line?" Elba asked. "If the Grand Wizard dies, does the magic pass to him?"

"I don't think so," Kip said. "I knew the GW had a daughter. That must be Lawrence's mother."

Elba looked between the two of them. "So, where's she?"

"Good question." Hem sighed. "Maybe she's the leader of the Freedoms. Lawrence told us he wasn't."

Elba squeezed Kip's hand. "What are we going to do?"

He looked at her, pain shimmering in his silver eyes. "What do you think we should do?"

Elba frowned, glancing at Hem, who shrugged in return. "The way I see it, you have three options: Message Lawrence and take him up on his offer to keep us safe. Turn ourselves in to the bureau and hope they don't incinerate us, or run away and hope no one ever finds us."

Hem snorted. "As fun as life on the run with you two sounds, I vote we message Lawrence."

Kip gave a small nod, but kept his gaze fixed on the floor, his brow furrowed.

"I know this sucks hard," Hem said, shuffling forward and putting a hand on his friend's shoulder, "but we need to face facts. The bureau lied to us. They lied to everyone. We've thought Pearson was a dick ever since we were kids. Now we know our gut instinct was right."

"Message him, then," Kip said. "There's no going back to the bureau even if we wanted to. I know that."

Elba's heart ached at his tone—at the slump in his shoulders. Every truth they uncovered was a knife to his soul. She wished there was something she could do to ease the pain knotted in his chest.

"Done," Hem announced, slamming the pen down on the

side. "Is anyone else hoping that their HQ is a private yacht in the Bahamas?"

Elba smiled, appreciating his relentless attempts to keep Kip from his downward spiral. "I don't know," she said. "I think I'd prefer a private island. No sea sickness."

"Good point," Hem said, his eyes fixed on Kip's bowed head. With a small sigh, he picked up the paper. "I'll let you know when he responds."

The faintest fizzle of magic rippled in the air and Elba gasped. "Did you feel that?"

"Yes," Kip said, looking at her. "It's weird that you did, though."

Hem held out the paper. "It's Lawrence. He wants us to tell him where we are. Says to pack up and they'll be here within five minutes of telling him."

Elba looked around the sparse room. "You might as well tell him now. It looks like none of us really bothered unpacking."

Hem looked at Kip for confirmation and then snatched up the pen and wrote down the address and room number of the hotel.

"Fuck!" Elba exclaimed. "What about Siena?"

Hem paused, pen in hand, his mouth open. "Shit."

"The bureau doesn't even know she exists," Kip reasoned. "She should be safe here."

Elba stood, shaking her head. "We can't just leave her. How would we even begin to explain it?"

She jolted as a knock sounded on the door.

"Lawrence already?" Hem raised his eyebrows as he moved to open it.

It wasn't Lawrence or his people. Instead, Siena stood, dressed in a smart cream suit, sky high beige heels highlighting her tanned calves. How she'd gone from dishevelled to cover model in such a short space of time, Elba couldn't begin to fathom.

"My room is on the floor below," Siena said, looking up from her phone. "Number sixteen. The office seems to think it will be a late one. There's been a big problem they need me to help with. By the time I get back it will be evening, and I could really do with an early night after the flight. Shall we regroup tomorrow?"

Elba walked to the door. "That sounds great. There's no rush, right?"

"Exactly." Siena smiled. "From the way my new boss sounded, I think I'll be here for a while."

She leaned forward and kissed Elba on each cheek before lifting her hand in a wave to the others. "Stay out of trouble."

Hem closed the door with a snort. "Says the woman shagging the hotel staff in someone else's room."

"Sounds like something you'd do, to be fair," Kip said, his mouth twitching. "In fact. I'm pretty sure you've done that several times."

Hem pointedly ignored him, turning to Elba instead. "I guess we pack then. Grab your stuff we'll meet back here."

Less than ten minutes later, Elba had just placed her packed bag down on Hem's bed when a knock sounded at the door. Black smoke unfurled at his wrists, matching the flickers of silver flame encircling Kip's fingers as they moved toward it.

One of them—she couldn't be sure who—sent magic forward to open the door, revealing two men and a woman dressed casually in jeans and sweatshirts.

"Lawrence sent us," the black-haired man at the front said. "Let's go."

Elba shot Kip a nervous glance, finding his jaw set as he eyed the people in the doorway.

"Can you tell us anything?" Hem asked, his tone clear he wasn't expecting an answer.

The man stared, his expression blank. Hem hoisted his bag onto his shoulder, giving them a brief glance before gripping hold of the man's outstretched forearm. A whip of pale blue flame enveloped them, and they were gone.

Kip took hold of Elba's hand and tugged her forward. She could barely breathe as she took hold of the small blonde haired woman's arm and a shimmering mist closed in around her.

When the mist cleared, Elba blinked at the plain lobby surrounding her. A bored security guard sat flipping through a magazine, not even lifting his eyes to look at the six people who had just appeared on the dark red, patterned carpet.

"This way," the man who'd magicked Kip said.

They followed him as he strode towards a fire escape, shooting each other curious expressions. The man led them downwards and Elba noted that the other two didn't follow behind. Perhaps it was a show of trust—that they were guests, not prisoners.

After descending only one floor, the man pushed open a door leading to a long corridor. Their footsteps echoed on the concrete, the only other sound the humming of the thin florescent lights above them. Elba shifted her heavy bag on her shoulder and tried not to look along the dark corners and crevices, sure she'd see rats, spiders, or something else that would cause her to squeal.

Just as she summoned the courage to ask how much further it would be, they reached another identical fire escape door. The man pushed it open and they made their way up two flights of concrete stairs. When they stepped through a door into another lobby, she almost gasped as she realised they'd travelled under the streets.

This was a very different building to the last. The carpet beneath them was a plush navy blue, enclosed by walls of dark polished wood. Gold lighting fixtures hung from the high ceiling, adorned with delicate glass globes, and a receptionist grinned at them from behind a desk that gleamed as bright as her shining dark brown bob.

"Welcome," she said, her teeth blinding white. "How many rooms do you require?"

Elba raised her eyebrows in surprise. This was a hotel? She glanced at their guide, but his dark eyes revealed nothing as he awaited their response.

"Two please," Hem said.

The receptionist held out two gold key cards. "Eleventh floor," she said. "Someone will be in touch soon."

Their guide stalked over to a bank of elevators and pressed the up button before disappearing in a plume of deep red sparks.

"He was chatty," Elba said, eyeing the fading embers as they sank into the carpet.

Hem chuckled as the doors pinged open and they stepped inside. "What do you reckon?"

"This feels wrong," Kip said, his words clipped.

Elba reached up and stroked his arm. "Things have felt wrong for a while, haven't they?"

He frowned, but his expression softened as he looked at her, the tension in his shoulders easing just a fraction. "I suppose."

They reached the eleventh floor and Hem eyed his key card before leaning across to look at the one in Kip's hand. "Oh, great," he moaned. "Our rooms are next to each other."

Elba rolled her eyes as they padded down the carpeted hallway. "No, they're not. You're across the hall."

Hem fist pumped the air and she laughed.

"Do you think people are in these rooms?" Kip asked, eyeing the gold numbers on the shiny doors.

Hem frowned. "No idea. I mean, what is this place? Is it a random hotel? Is it the Freedom headquarters? Where the fuck is Lawrence?"

"I don't think it's a random hotel," Elba replied. "Not with people magicking in and out in the foyer."

Kip paused in front of a door, swiping the key through the lock. It blinked green and he pushed it open.

"Holy shit," Hem muttered from behind them. "I'm going to check mine out."

Elba didn't respond as she stepped into the room, Kip behind her. Floor to ceiling windows lined an entire wall, providing a view of the city, sprawled out below them. She dropped her bag onto the enormous bed that took up most of the other wall, running her fingers over the expensive furniture and fixtures as she walked to the window. There was something about the room that gave just the right touch of elegance amidst the modern feel.

"This is not the eleventh floor," Kip said, his hands in his pockets as he surveyed the view. "The elevator must be fixed to skip floors."

"Perhaps that's where the headquarters are," Elba mused, her eyes fixed on the skyscrapers obscuring the winding river in the distance.

Elba jumped at the firm knock at the door, cursing her racing pulse as Kip went to answer it. It was most likely Hem coming to compare the view from his side of the building.

"I hope the room is to your liking?"

Kip stepped back to allow Lawrence into the room. "It's not the eleventh floor."

"I think what Kip means to say is, it's lovely, thank you," Elba said, shooting him a look. If they were going to be staying with the Freedoms, they'd have to start trusting them, at least a little.

Lawrence gave her a grateful smile, inclining his head. "You're welcome. And you're right. This isn't technically the eleventh floor."

"No shit," Hem said, appearing behind him. "What floor is it really?"

"Thirty-third, I believe," Lawrence said, glancing out the window.

"What's on the floors we skipped?" Kip asked.

"That's why I came here." He glanced around, before sitting on the edge of the bed. "I know you don't trust us, but I wanted to give you something to think about."

"Oh?" Hem folded his arms across his chest.

Lawrence pulled a hand over his face. "You've been told these past few years that we want to wipe out Normals and practise our magic freely. I need you to know that is what the bureau wanted you to believe. It's that sort of propaganda that has made our job so hard. Yes. We want freedom, but not in that way."

"The restrictors?" Elba asked.

Lawrence nodded. "Exactly. That's how it all started. We found out about the restrictors and when the Grand Wizard tried to regain control, they anticipated it. They used ancient artefacts and managed to capture him." He shook his head. "The restrictors are just the beginning. There is so much the bureau—the First Tier—has done."

"What's your goal, then?" Kip asked. "To take down the First Tier?"

Lawrence stared up at them, fierce determination in his eyes. "Yes. That and rescue my grandfather before it's too late."

"Do you know where they have him?" Elba asked.

He shook his head. "No. We're fairly certain he's not at the bureau, but we've been unable to locate him. The only thing we're certain of, is that he's still alive."

"Because if he died, his power would pass on," Kip said.

Lawrence nodded. "She's not in town at the moment, but my mother wants to meet with you tomorrow."

"Why us?" Kip asked, gesturing to the group. "I'm assuming you don't go to this much trouble for all your new recruits?"

Elba raised her eyebrows. She hadn't even considered they were being treated any differently. Perhaps they weren't.

After all, if Lawrence was as rich as they said he was, this room might be standard.

Lawrence rubbed his palms on his thighs before standing. "I understand that everything you've ever known has been called in to question. I really do. However, this is bigger than just the bureau. My entire life has been about the future of magic. One day, when my mother dies, I will become the conduit through which all the world's magic will flow. I've known this since I was old enough to conjure my first spark, but it doesn't make it any less terrifying. I'm expected to have a child, so that the legacy can continue. This is my life. My duty. I'll do anything I have to, to protect magic."

"What would happen if you didn't have a child?" Elba asked, trying to imagine the weight of the burden on this normal looking man's shoulders.

Lawrence gave her a pained look. "Experts say that magic would die. It would evaporate into the ether. The truth is, no one knows."

"That's a lot of pressure," Elba said, sympathy weighing heavy on her chest.

He gave her a small smile before turning back to Kip and Hem. "The reason I was so keen to recruit you two, is because of your standing. You might not have known Naomi, but she knew you. We have your files."

Elba watched as Hemingway and Kipling visibly tensed, half expecting smoke and flame to ripple at their fingertips.

"And?" Hem asked. "What did our files tell you?"

Lawrence tucked his hands in his pockets and shook his head. "A lot. I'll share them with you tomorrow. You know what I'm talking about though. You both applied to join the Second Tier twice and were turned down both times."

Hem grunted. "Thanks for bringing that up."

"It's fine. We don't like paperwork," Kip bit out.

Lawrence shook his head. "There's a reason the First Tier didn't want to promote you. Why they wanted to hold you back. It's the same reason we wanted you to join us. You're the best they have, and they knew that if you got close enough to finding out what was going on, you'd stop it. That's all I want from you. To help stop it."

Lawrence's words hung heavy in the air, cushioned by silence, until he moved toward the door. "As I said, I wanted to give you something to think about. Take tonight. Order anything you want to the room and it will be taken care of."

Without another word, he turned and left, closing the door behind him with a soft click.

Elba watched as Hem and Kip stared into the distance, their faces wearing identical frowns. "How many tiers are there?" she asked.

Kip blinked, turning to her. "Pardon?"

"If that Pearson guy and his team stopped you from being promoted to the Second Tier, that means you're Third Tier, right?"

"Sure," Kip answered, the corners of his mouth twitching.

"So," Elba continued, "how many tiers are there?"

"Twenty-two," Kip replied, not bothering to hide the pride in his voice.

Elba's jaw dropped. "Twenty-two? How is that even possible? What are the people on the bottom tier doing?"

Hem chuckled. "The Twenty-Seconds are the newbs—the kids brought in by the bureau."

"Still," Elba said. "That's pretty impressive."

Kip let his frown fall into a grin and wrapped his arms around her. "Thank you."

She knew he wasn't just talking about the compliment. "Why don't we take advantage of this incredible room and order some food?"

"I'll see you guys later," Hem said, moving to the door.

"Woah there, cowboy." Elba reached out and grabbed hold of his sleeve. "I meant all three of us. Let's talk about what you want to do and maybe even take a minute to relax."

Hem glanced at Kip before back to her. "I figured you guys would want to test out the bed."

"For fucksake, Hem." Kip chuckled, shoving his shoulder. "We're not horny teenagers. I can restrain myself until later."

His fingers tightened around her waist at the promise of later and Elba shivered under his touch.

"Fine," Hem said, rooting for a menu. "Let's see if the menu is as posh as the rooms."

"What would satisfy that criteria?" Elba asked, peering over his shoulder as he pulled a leather bound file from the dresser.

Hem frowned as he trailed a finger down the menu. "Lobster."

"Lobster?" Kip echoed. "You have a shellfish allergy."

Hem looked up with a grin. "I didn't say I was going to eat it."

"You can't do that," Elba gasped, snatching the menu from his hands.

"Hey!" Hem protested trying to wrestle it back from her. "I didn't say I was going to order it either. I just wanted to see how posh this place is."

"Fine." Elba handed him back the menu with narrowed eyes.

Hem snatched it from her, shooting her a withering look. "I will, however, be ordering their most expensive bottle of champagne."

EIGHTEEN

RINSING THE SINK, Elba glanced in the mirror to check she hadn't splattered toothpaste across her face. Kip strode into the bathroom and slipped his hands around her waist, resting his chin on her shoulder.

"You okay?" he asked.

She turned her head to nuzzle her nose against the faint beginnings of stubble on his cheek. "Considering we're on the run from what seems to be a group of evil power-hungry psychopaths, I'm pretty okay."

Kip huffed a laugh, his breath tickling her neck. "I think I'm feeling a bit more grounded about it now."

"Really?" Elba held his gaze in the mirror. "That's good. What changed?"

He pressed a kiss against her cheek before straightening and turning her to face him. "I think I was spiralling because the idea of the bureau—the entirety of the Men of Magic—being evil, was too much to take in. It's been my entire life since I was a kid. If what Lawrence is saying is true, it's not everything. It's just Pearson and the rest of the First Tier."

Elba pulled her lip under her teeth, relief filling her lungs. "I think he's telling the truth," she said.

"He probably is," Kip admitted. "I'm not going to let my guard down for either side, though."

Reaching up, Elba stroked her fingers down the side of his face. How was it she was still in awe of how gorgeous he was? His magic thrummed under her skin and she wondered what would happen if she released a little and let it flicker across his skin.

Kip closed his eyes as he turned his head into her hand, pressing a kiss against her palm. "What are you thinking?"

Elba blinked, her cheeks heating. "I was thinking it's been a really long day."

"Tired?"

She considered the question, and the other question it held, shimmering in his eyes. Her mind had started replaying the events of the day, however, and she frowned.

"You like modern art."

Kip raised his eyebrows, his mouth curving into a smile. "Random, but okay. Yes. I mean, I like a lot of art. Not just modern."

She shook her head. "Yet you had those awful prints in your apartment. Why?"

His eyes shuttered as he looked away. "You know why."

Elba's chest tightened as she looked up at him. He'd been happy and she'd chased it away. Her mind grasped at ways to try and bring that beautiful smile back.

"Who was that artist you said you wanted to see?" she asked. "What kind of art do they . . . make? Paint? Create? What do you say?" Perhaps it would have been easier to just take off her sweater.

The corner of Kip's mouth pulled. "Christy Lee Rogers. She's a Hawaiian photographer and artist. Her work is . . ."

Elba smiled as he struggled to find the words. "You'll have to take me when all this is over."

"Yeah." His handsome face fell into a frown, his mouth moving as though deep in thought.

"What?"

When he looked at her, the mischievous glint in his silver eyes stopped her breath in her lungs. "What about now?"

Elba looked at her watch. "It's half eleven," she said. "The museum will have closed hours ago."

"Exactly." Kip's eyes flashed.

She gasped, giving his chest a gentle shove. "Are you suggesting we break in?"

"Is it breaking in if we don't use the door?" he asked, raising his dark eyebrows.

A laugh gathered in her throat. "What about guards? CCTV? We already have enough people after us without the Normal police, too."

"Do you trust me?" Kip said, taking her hands in his and pulling them to his chest.

Elba smiled, squeezing his fingers. "Yes. Of course."

In response, silver flames encircled them, stealing the tiled floor from beneath their feet.

As the museum materialised around them, Elba pressed herself against Kip, her eyes wide. He'd brought them back to where they'd met Lawrence, the tree sculpture sending eerie shadows across the walls like elongated fingers. It was deathly silent, and the only light was that of the green emergency exit lights at the doorways.

"How do we look at art in the dark?" she whispered.

Kip took her hand in his and tugged her towards the door Lawrence had left through. The hallway split into two sections and after squinting at a sign, he turned right.

"Her exhibit should be in here," he said, almost to himself.

Excitement flickered in her limbs, dancing with his magic as she watched his focus with a smile.

"Here we go," he breathed, coming to a stop. He muttered a spell and the room lit with a soft light; his own face illuminated with something that looked like pure joy.

Elba tore her gaze from his face, her own eyes widening as

she let her hand fall from his and took a step toward one the enormous canvases filling the space. At first, the swirls of bright colour seemed just that, but as she watched, they formed writhing bodies, draped in colourful material swirling beneath water.

"She uses a mixture of photography and painting," Kip explained at her ear.

Elba nodded, moving on to the next piece. Three women surrounded by teal coloured water, the flow of material around them representing so much movement and emotion, she felt her chest tighten.

"They're really something, aren't they?" Kip said, pressing a kiss to her cheek before moving on to take in another piece.

"They're stunning," she breathed, her eyes drinking in the light and shade filtering through the rippling fabric as though she could see it moving.

Kip moved to stand behind her, slipping his arms around her waist. "If we make it out of this alive, maybe I'll buy one."

She turned to look up at him. "Can you do that?"

"What? Buy one? Of course."

Elba bit her lip as she turned back to the canvas. She couldn't ask him how much it would cost. If he and Hem really were so high up in the bureau, they must be getting paid quite well, and it wasn't like he spent his money on anything she could see.

"I can practically hear the gears in your brain whirring." Kip chuckled at her ear. "Spit it out."

She turned in his arms, encircling his waist. "I was wondering what you spend your money on other than expensive suits. Do you have a sports car hidden away somewhere?"

"A car?" Kip pulled a face. "No. I don't even know how to drive."

"What? Really?"

"Why would I learn to drive when I can magic anywhere I want to?"

Elba frowned. "I suppose so. What then? Do you have a drawer of watches somewhere? An expensive bourbon collection?"

As soon as the words left her lips, she realised that if he had any of those things, they were most likely gone now. His smile didn't fade however as he looked down at her.

"No. You called it with the suits, I suppose. I'll have to re-buy them all now, but I had a nice little collection."

Elba ran her hands across his chest. "You never let yourself splurge?"

"Not really," he said. "I mean, Hem and I like to try nice restaurants and stuff. There's always been work, though."

"Wait. Surely even Men get holidays?"

Kip shrugged. "I mean, we can put in requests I suppose."

Her mouth fell open. "Kipling Solum, when was the last time you went on holiday?"

He frowned, looking past her at the artwork as he considered. "Hem and I went to the South of France about six years ago."

She matched his frown. "Was that a holiday or still work?"

"A working holiday?"

Elba smacked his chest and he laughed until she shushed him. "Won't people hear?"

He slid his hands along her arms, the laughter lingering in his eyes. "The spell I cast muffles the sound. You said you trusted me."

"I do." She reached up and trailed her fingers along the side of his neck and along his collarbone. "I want you to take a holiday."

"I'm a little bit busy at the moment," he said, his own fingers tracing down her back. "I don't think Lawrence would appreciate me jetting off right now."

Elba rose up on her tiptoes and pressed a kiss to his cheek.

"When all this is over. I want you to buy yourself a piece of art and take a holiday."

Kip stared down at her, his hands brushing up her arms until they framed her face. He leaned forward and pressed a kiss to her forehead. "Fine." A kiss to her nose. "On one condition."

"What?" she breathed as he hovered his mouth over hers.

"You'll come with me."

His breath was warm on her lips as his magic called to hers like static electricity beneath her skin. "Do you feel that?"

"Yes," he whispered. "Are you avoiding the question?"

Elba reached up, entwining her fingers in his thick, dark curls. "Of course, I'll come with you."

She caught a glimpse of his smile before Kip closed the gap between them, his lips brushing hers as his hands pressed her against him.

"Am I turning you on?" he asked.

Elba blinked. "Excuse me?"

Kip's smile stretched into a grin as he trailed a finger along her neck. "You're on fire."

Glancing down, Elba's eyes widened at the faint flickers of pale flame across her skin.

"Do you remember?" he asked. "That first night at your apartment, when you played with my flames?" Kip dipped his fingertips through her sparks, sending shivers across her skin.

Elba's heart raced, both at the feeling and the memory. She opened her mouth to respond, but she reached up and pulled his face to hers instead, claiming his lips.

Her body melted into his touch and she allowed her flames of magic to reach out to his. Silver fire flickered along her skin as she slid her hands under Kip's sweater, her fingers desperate for his skin. He moaned against her mouth, his tongue sweeping hers as his fingers tugged at her top.

Kip stepped away from her and she gasped, wondering if she'd done something wrong. Instead, he gripped the bottom of his sweater and pulled it off over his head, dropping it on the floor. Elba didn't allow herself to think—to question whether this was a good idea or not—before doing the same with her own.

He met her gaze for a split second before rushing toward her, his kiss frenzied as he pushed her back until they met the wall. When his lips moved from her mouth to her neck, Elba opened her eyes long enough to see silver flames covering his skin in a faint silver haze, his magic blurring with her own. She leaned her head back and sighed at the feeling. It was as though the magic he was sharing with her wanted to merge with his. It felt like being whole.

Kip's hands unclasped her bra and, letting it fall to the ground, his fingers and tongue found her breasts. Fisting her hands in his hair, Elba arched against him, and as his mouth claimed hers once more, his fingers slipped inside her jeans, easing them down over her hips. She hadn't even noticed him undoing them. Barely breaking their kiss, she kicked out of them as he unfastened and shimmied out of his own.

Elba's head spun, drunk on the sensation of their mingling magic and the heady passion of his touch, his mouth. She wondered if he felt the same, too lost in the feeling to magic their clothes away. Kip's lips moved in a whisper against her neck and when she opened her eyes, the white stone bench before the artwork had transformed into a pile of soft grey blankets. He tugged her down toward them, his hands caressing her back as he eased her down.

Holding himself over her, his chest heaved, his pupils blown. "Do you feel it?" he breathed.

"Yes." Elba knew he was talking about the licks of silver flame reaching up from her body, tangling and twisting with his, causing every atom of her body to light up like fireworks.

She swallowed, her own breathing ragged, as she trailed her fingers through the flames.

She leaned up to take his mouth with hers and he nudged her legs apart, pressing into her. With each gradual push, he deepened the kiss—the urgent sweeping of his tongue a stark contrast to the gentle slowness with which he entered her. When he was buried inside her, he broke their kiss, resting his forehead against hers. Elba whimpered at the pause, wrapping her leg around him to angle him even deeper.

Kip trembled as he held her gaze. She knew he was trying to make it last, but the push and pull of magic between them was all consuming. She knew she'd be undone in seconds. He hooked her leg with his arm and with a shaking breath, withdrew before slamming back into her.

Elba couldn't bite back her cry as he gathered pace, her body exploding with the sensation. She reached for his face, kissing him hard before shoving him off her. The shock on his face lasted less than a second as she pushed him onto his back and straddled him.

The moan that escaped her as she slid onto him caused Kip to grasp her ass, his fingers gripping so tight she whimpered. Before she could move them, he slid them to her hips, holding her steady as she began to move. One hand reached for the scar on her breast, now glowing in an almost neon blue.

Kip's body was starlight beneath the swathes of silver flame as he arched beneath her, his head thrown back and his jaw clenched. Elba slid her hands down the grooves of his muscled chest, her fingers gripping his skin as her pleasure jolted through her in waves. Kip moaned her name as a faint golden shimmer lit his skin beneath the flames.

For several minutes, as she lay on Kip's chest, the only sound their tandem breathing as the flames winked out, leaving them in the soft lighting of the gallery.

"You are so fucking beautiful," Kip whispered, his fingers

stroking her spine. "And that was . . . There are no words for what that was."

Elba pressed a kiss to his chest as he pulled the blankets over them. "Why didn't that happen at the hotel?"

"I don't know. Perhaps it's because you're beginning to wield magic more confidently—like it's becoming a part of you."

Elba watched as Kip reached up and traced the lines of the scar, now only a faint blue. "Do you think it will stay?" she asked.

"I have no idea. I mean, scars can fade. It's not been there for very long. I suppose we have to wait and see."

"Do you mind?" Elba forced herself to meet his gaze, her heart racing. "Sharing your magic with me?"

Kip smiled, perhaps sensing her nerves, and pressed a kiss to her lips. "No. I don't. I can't even tell. I mean, I'm not used to this new super-charged power yet anyway, but even if I was, I wouldn't mind."

"What if it doesn't go away?" she asked, her throat growing dry. "How far away from each other do you think we can go before the link breaks?"

Kip wrapped his arms around her and squeezed. "We'll deal with that when we have to, and as for how far away we can go? I have no plans to put any distance between us, so if you want to test that, you're going to have to let me know."

Elba smiled, although the nerves still writhed in her belly. Despite the way she felt about him, Kip had proven time and time again that he could go from hot to cold in an instant. She wanted to trust him, but he'd have to earn it, and that took time.

"I mean it," he said, the smile slipping from his face as he watched the doubt in her eyes.

Elba pressed her lips to his. "I know."

NINETEEN

THEY WOKE to Hem hammering on their door, a message from Lawrence in his hands asking what they'd decided. Elba knew Kipling that was the most reluctant to let go of the bureau, but he still agreed it was the right move. The bureau was out for their blood, and life on the run was not an attractive option. It made sense to find out what Lawrence had to tell them.

He'd sent a representative to collect them at nine and Elba was grateful of the lie-in after the late night at the museum. A flutter of electricity shivered across her skin as she followed the tall brunette escorting them to Lawrence. Whatever had happened between her and Kip and their shared magic had been indescribable.

Kip brushed his fingers against hers and her chest contracted as she glanced up at him. She'd caught him giving her strange looks all morning and she was fairly certain it had to do with what he'd said about not putting distance between them. Elba didn't doubt that he believed it, but it was just too hard to believe after the events of the last few days.

Seven of the floors between the foyer and the 'hotel' rooms were dedicated to Lawrence's people and as their footsteps echoed down the long hallway, the décor of the hotel faded into something distinctly more corporate. Elba's heart rate quickened as they slowed before a large set of deep red doors. The brunette barely paused before shoving them open.

Elba baulked as their escort stood back to let them enter what appeared to be an enormous control room. Lawrence stood before large screens that covered two of the walls, displaying various maps and photos. Desks and computers were scattered around the room, occupied by dozens of men and women. Some were dressed casually in jeans and sweat-shirts, whereas others were dressed in leathers and combats like Selena and Naomi had been when they'd first broken into her apartment. She pushed down the involuntary shudder that tickled her spine.

"Good morning. I trust you slept well?" Lawrence asked stepping forward. "Welcome to our headquarters."

Elba stole a glance at Kip and Hem to find them staring at their surroundings with a mix of awe and disbelief. It was a huge leap of faith for Lawrence to share this with them.

Hem let out a low whistle. "This is pretty impressive."

"The Grand Wizard has a lot of supporters," Lawrence admitted. "We were cautious about reaching out to other chapters of Men, but we recently brought three countries on board and it's been extremely useful."

"What exactly do you do here?" Elba asked, craning her neck to look at the screens.

Lawrence motioned for them to follow him over to one of the large monitors. He pointed at a list of information displayed along the left-hand side. "This is a list of known conduit stones and their last known locations and owners. We have teams trying to track them down. As you know, it can be quite dangerous."

Elba stared at the screen. Professor Hendy's stone had been on that list not so long ago, sending Kipling and Hemingway spiralling into her life.

A set of doors at the other end of the room opened and a group of people dressed in black spilled in, causing Hem and Kip to tense, magic sparking at their fingertips.

"At ease, gentlemen," the woman at the head of the crowd said, her eyebrows raised as she took in the spirals of smoke and flickers of flame.

Elba watched as she stepped forward, the other men and women falling into place behind her. She looked to be in her sixties, with long white-grey hair tied in a high ponytail that draped down her shoulder to her waist. Dressed elegantly in a navy pantsuit that highlighted her eyes, she had a confidence about her that commanded the room. Elba stared at her, feeling her magic pulsing as though responding to the woman's presence.

"Elba, Kipling, Hemingway," Lawrence said, gesturing to the woman. "This is my mother, Lindsey. Heir to the Grand Wizard and all magic."

Kip and Hem immediately dropped to their knees, their heads bowed, and Elba's eyes widened, unsure whether to do the same, as the woman looked them over.

When Lindsey's dark blue eyes landed on her, she felt her magic swell in response. Maybe it was more than her presence, perhaps her magic was responding to the fact that this woman was the next living conduit for the entire world's magic. Elba had already noted that Lawrence seemed effortlessly powerful. Just how powerful was his mother?

"You're different," Lindsey said, taking a step closer to her.

Kip raised his head, his eyes fixed on the heir. "It's an honour to meet you."

She smiled at Kip before returning her gaze to Elba. "You have magic."

The room had fallen silent. Somehow the bustle and ringing of phones had faded to nothingness, highlighting the pounding of her heart inside her chest. Lindsey, the heir, knew. She knew she was a Normal with magic. Elba looked to Kip, who was staring up at Lindsey, his jaw set.

"Of course, she has magic," Hem said, breaking the silence. "We all have magic."

"Stand. Please." Lindsey tore her gaze from Elba, her frown deepening as she looked Hem up and down. "I understand that you are skittish and that you still don't trust us, but lying to our faces will not benefit anyone."

Hem's fists clenched at his sides, the tension thickening until it was almost suffocating.

Lawrence stepped forward, giving Elba an apologetic smile. "As I mentioned, we know who you all are. We knew of Kipling and Hemingway through Selena but once we discovered you were involved, Elba, we did some research."

Elba's eyes widened. "What kind of research?"

"Just the basics," Lawrence said, nodding at a woman near a computer. She tapped a few keys and one of the large screens flickered into an information file.

Elba's mouth opened as she stared up at her passport photo, accompanied by a few more recent CCTV frames of her walking to work or from the gym. All her information was there. Her birthday. Her address. Her parents. Even her blood type.

"You're a Normal," Lindsey said. "You shouldn't have magic, yet I can feel it."

Elba met the woman's narrowed gaze and swallowed. She knew. There was no point lying her way out of it. "We used a conduit stone to give me magic so I could help with Selena's rescue," she explained.

Lawrence frowned. "You said the bureau took the stone."

Deciding it would be easier to show them rather than explain, Elba tugged down the front of her top to show the glowing blue scar half hidden by her bra.

"Well, that's different," Lindsey breathed, stepping closer. "And you can wield?"

In answer, Elba commanded a burst of silver flames to her fingers.

"Whose magic are you wielding?" she asked, her eyes fixed on the flickering flames.

"Kipling's," Elba answered, recalling the flames. She turned to him, but he was still focused on the heir and her grandson, his silver gaze assessing and monitoring their every breath.

"Elba?" Lawrence stepped closer. "How would you feel about letting some of our team take a look at you to figure out how it's working?"

"Absolutely not," Kip answered, his words clipped.

Elba raised her eyebrows. She wasn't planning on agreeing to it, but there was also no way she was going to have someone answering for her. "I can answer for myself, thank you."

Kip finally looked at her, uncertainty flickering beneath the anger in his eyes.

"I'd rather not, for now," Elba said, turning back to Lawrence.

Lindsey folded her arms. "Do the bureau know about your magic?"

Elba blinked. The Men had seen her wield flames after taking the stone. "Possibly."

Lawrence and Lindsey shared a look.

"What?" Kip asked. "Why does that matter?"

Lawrence gestured to the doors his mother had entered through. "Let's go and talk somewhere more private."

Elba swallowed, her nerves twisting her stomach. Kip placed his hand on the small of her back and she leaned into his touch. Whatever they had to say, it wasn't going to be good.

They followed Lawrence, Lindsey, and what must have been her security team, through the doors and along a sparse corridor. Elba wondered whether Siena was awake yet. She hoped she was having a lie in. At some point, she'd have to get hold of a new phone or ask Lawrence's team if they could make hers secure.

The group came to a halt and Elba almost walked into the back of one of the black-clad minions as they stopped to open a door. Filing into a large meeting room, Lindsay slid into the leather chair at the head of the table, Lawrence took the seat to her left, and gestured for them to sit down. The others stayed outside, closing the door behind them.

"I'll stand, if that's okay," Hem said, folding his arms.

Lawrence braced his arms on the table, glancing between them, annoyance creasing his brow. "You really aren't going to make this easy, are you?"

"Freedoms have murdered dozens of our friends and colleagues over the last few years," Hem said through gritted teeth.

A fine pale mist appeared around Lindsey's hands as she gripped her arms. "Do you know how many of our people have died at the hands of the bureau? Not just murdered, but imprisoned, tortured and then butchered."

"At least any Men we killed died a swift death," Lawrence added.

"Swift?" Kip spat. "Is that what Naomi was doing to me?"

Lindsey raised an eyebrow at Lawrence who fixed his pale blue gaze on the table. Elba looked between them. Did Lindsey not know what Naomi had done?

"Look," Lawrence ground out. "This is war. There have been casualties on both sides but, with your help, we can finally end it. You have to start trusting us, though. We've shown you our headquarters. We've not withheld anything from you."

It was true, Elba realised. She sank down into one of the seats around the table, ignoring the eyes on her back. "What did you want to say to us that couldn't be said in the other room?"

"You could be in danger," Lindsey said. "Much greater danger than you think you are at the moment."

"If the bureau knows that you're a conduit," Lawrence continued, "they'll want you."

Elba frowned, turning to Kip and Hem as they reluctantly sank down on the seats on either side of her. "Why?"

"A conduit stone allows a wielder to control between ten and twenty percent of a person's magic," Lawrence explained. "If my suspicions are correct, you are now a living conduit. You might be able to channel infinitely more than a stone."

"And if the bureau got hold of you," Lindsey said, holding her gaze, "they could use you to channel my father's magic. There's a possibility they wouldn't need the rest of the stones if they had you."

Elba's stomach somersaulted and Kip's hand slid to her thigh, gripping gently.

Hem leaned back in his chair. "This is all speculation, though. Elba might be able to channel magic, but for all we know, the mark is just a lingering ghost of the conduit stone's abilities. It might be gone by tomorrow."

Elba fought the urge to touch the mark beneath her top—tried not to think about how it would feel to wake up and not feel Kip's magic flowing beneath her skin. What if they could never recreate what happened between them last night? Elba's fingers tightened into fists on her lap. It had only been a couple of days, but already she didn't want to let her magic go. But then, it wasn't her magic. It was Kip's.

"This is why we wanted to run some tests," Lawrence explained. "I've never seen or heard of anything like it before."

"Neither have I," Lindsay said. "It's remarkable. Exactly how much of Kipling's power can you wield?"

Elba glanced down at her hands. "I don't know. We haven't really had the time to test it out properly."

"What does it feel like?" Lawrence asked, looking at Kip. "Does it feel like she's draining your power?"

Elba's stomach flipflopped at the term. Was she? She turned to Kip who in return, tightened his grip on her thigh.

"No," he said. "It doesn't."

Lindsey leaned back in her chair, the squeak of the leather amidst the tense silence loud enough to make Elba flinch. "Would you be willing to send as much magic as you can to that far wall? See if you can bring it down?"

Elba baulked. "Excuse me?"

"She's not a performing monkey," Kip snapped.

Lawrence sighed, pulling a hand across his face. "Kipling, I don't think you realise quite how serious this is. If we're correct—if Elba really can be utilised as a human conduit—the bureau will stop at nothing to get hold of her."

A shiver traced down Elba's spine. She loved the feeling of Kip's magic but now, a part of her wanted to claw the scar from her skin. "I'd like to try," she whispered. "I want to know."

Lindsey gave her a tight smile. "Good. Don't worry about damage. This room is warded. Even if you broke down the wall, it wouldn't hurt or damage anyone on the other side."

"What about Kip, though?" Elba asked, turning to him. The concern in his pale eyes caused her chest to tighten. "If you're right, will I hurt him?"

"If it does feel like you're draining me, I'll tell you and you can stop," Kip said. "Are you sure you want to do this?"

Elba nodded. "Yes."

Her legs trembling, she got to her feet, already summoning the rippling magic beneath her skin. Turning to the far wall, she commanded the flames to her raised fingers, imagining powerful jets of water, strong enough to blast through brick. Power shot out with enough force to cause her to take a step to brace herself. The flames hit the wall with a groan, but she kept pushing. Pulling and pulling on the power, she felt it this time—syphoning through the thin thread connecting her to Kip like a fine hose.

As a crack began to appear along the wall, she dared a glance to her side at Kipling. His creamy skin had paled further, his fingers gripping the table as he grimaced.

With a gasp she recalled the magic, her head spinning as she collapsed back into her seat, reaching for him.

She lifted a trembling hand to his shoulder. "Are you okay?"

When he turned to her, his eyes were bright with fear. Not because of what had just happened, she realised, but because of what it meant.

"I was draining you, wasn't I?" she whispered. "I felt it."

"The magic I could sense in you," Lindsey said, leaning against the table, her long white hair sweeping forward, "was like a small pool. I suspect with the link between you, a little of Kipling's magic has spilled into you like an overflowing pool. When you actively pull, however, the link becomes a tap rather than overspill."

"Would it be possible to drain someone completely?" Hem asked.

Elba's eyes widened as she turned to Lindsey, who nodded grimly.

"Yes. It's very possible."

Elba stared down at her hands, her stomach roiling. "What would happen if you drained someone completely?"

Lindsey gave her a sympathetic smile. "If you drain someone of their magic, they die. Magical is intrinsic to us— part of our very being. Removing our magic would be like removing our heart."

Her own heart pounding in her ears, Elba lifted her gaze to Kip. She could have killed him. If she hadn't been able to recall the magic . . .

"I'm okay," Kip murmured, a small smile on his lips.

"You really think the bureau would use Elba to drain the GW?" Hem asked, pulling Elba's gaze.

Lawrence shared a pained look with his mother. "Possibly."

"I wouldn't do it, though," Elba said. "They couldn't make me."

Even as the words left her lips, she thought of the way the bureau treated their prisoners. They would go to any lengths to get what they wanted. Icy fear coated her skin as she thought of her family, her friends, being murdered by the bureau as punishment for fighting them. If they wanted to break her, there was a million different ways they could try.

Kip encased her trembling hand in hers, but she couldn't look at him as terror shook her to her core.

"We're still unsure what they actually plan to do," Lawrence said. "We've been unable to infiltrate that high up. It's actually why Selena was trying to recruit you. We'd hoped that you would have been able to find out."

Elba swallowed, her pulse still racing from the sensation of wielding so much magic and the thought of what it meant. Was Selena okay? She wondered whether the Freedoms knew with all their tracking technology.

"Wait," she said, a thought edging into her mind. "If I'm a human conduit, it means I pull power like the stone, right? Does it mean I can channel it to other people?"

Lawrence shared another look with Lindsey. "Possibly. I—"

His words were cut short by a cacophony of shouts and bangs somewhere on the other side of the door. Before Elba could draw a breath, Hem and Kip were on their feet, magic swirling at their wrists.

"Report!"

Elba snapped her gaze to Lindsey, who was standing, her dark eyes blazing and her phone to her ear. At her side, Lawrence's sparkling blue mist was eddying around him as he swiped at his own phone, his brow furrowed. Outside, shouts mixed with screams as the very walls seemed to vibrate alongside deafening booms.

Elba turned to Kip, her eyes wide. "What's going on?"

"It's the bureau," Lawrence said, cursing under his breath. "I don't know how they found us. There are so many wards . . . We've been so careful . . ."

Blood roared in Elba's ears as she looked at the power circling the men in the room, ready to face whatever tried to get in the room. It was only when she turned to Lindsey, she found the older woman watching her with narrowed eyes.

"You," she said. "Don't move."

Before Elba could respond, Lindsey summoned a small seed of red magic in her palm and sent it floating through the air towards her. It took Elba a second to recall it was similar to the one Hem used when he was trying to find the restrictor. Her breath caught in her throat. Did Lindsey think that she was responsible for this somehow?

The red light hovered above her head before moving downwards in a sweeping zigzagging motion. It didn't make it further than her neck before glowing brightly and disappearing.

"Shit." Hem muttered.

Elba turned to him with wild eyes. "What does that mean?"

"It means, somehow, the bureau planted a tracker in you," Kip said, his face pained. "We should have checked. We didn't think . . ."

"But when?" Elba's mind spun as she tried to think of how it could have happened.

"Bennet," Kip spat. "That fucking bastard."

Elba's fingers drifted to her neck. She'd felt his sparks burning her as he'd held her hostage. One of the sharp burning pains must have been the tracker. "Can we get it out?"

Lindsey held up a hand, a sharp knife appearing in her fingers.

Elba inhaled. "Seriously?"

"It won't be deep," Kip said, his fingers brushing against her neck. "I'll do it if you'll let me."

Flipping the knife in her hand, Lindsey held it out to Kip.

"Fine," Elba said, hoping she didn't look as terrified as she felt.

Kip pressed a kiss to her temple, brushing her hair away from her neck. "I'll be as quick as I can and I'll heal you right away, okay?"

Elba managed a nod and before she could prepare herself, she felt a sharp pain at the top of her shoulder. Just as it became too much to bear, the caress of Kip's magic swept warm against her skin and she exhaled.

"All done," he said, pressing a kiss to the spot.

She turned, staring at the tiny seed like object in his fingers, trying not to notice the blood—her blood—on its surface. Kip placed it on the table and smashed the hilt of the knife down on it.

A pained yell broke through the silence, and they all turned to the door.

"We should go and help," she said.

"No," Lawrence said, his eyes fixed on the door. "The guards outside wouldn't let us out even if we wanted to. They have orders to protect my mother and I at all costs. If we die or the bureau capture us . . ."

Elba swallowed, clenching and unclenching her fists at her side as his words trailed off, their meaning clear. The future of all magic was trapped in this seemingly ordinary boardroom, and in danger because of her.

"We also can't let them get hold of you," Lawrence said, causing her to turn.

"They're not getting anywhere near her," Kip said, his magic flaring at his fingertips.

"Not a chance," Hem said at her other side.

"Isn't there another way out of here?" Kip asked, scanning the room.

Lawrence shook his head. "No. Like I said, this place has evaded the bureau's knowledge for years. Every room is heavily warded but that's it."

"I can't believe we were stupid enough to allow ourselves to get in this situation," Lindsay snapped, shoving her chair back from the table.

"My mother and I are rarely in the same place at the same time," Lawrence explained, watching Lindsey's pacing. "In fact, this is probably the longest we've spent in the same room for at least eighteen months."

Lindsey paused in her pacing for a moment, pain flickering across her face. "We need to come up with a plan."

"If we can cause a distraction," Hem said, "would you be able to get out?"

"What do you mean?" Lawrence asked.

Elba turned to Hem, aware of the intense gaze Kip had fixed on him.

"Well, we've clocked that you're more powerful than the average Magic, Lawrence," Hem explained. "But, just how powerful are you, Lindsey?"

In response, white light flickered at her fingers, building until blinding orbs, humming with power encircled her forearms, bright enough that Elba had to turn away.

As she retracted her powers, admiration and awe painted Hem and Kip's faces. Elba blinked; the ghosts of the blazing power seared into her retinas. If Lindsey was that powerful, she couldn't begin to imagine how powerful the Grand Wizard was.

"Okay," Hem said, drawing a steadying breath. "The plan is that Kip, Elba and I will leave and try to draw them away while you make a run for it."

"No chance," Kip barked.

Hem gave Elba an apologetic glance before turning to him. "It's the future of all magic, mate. Either magic disappears forever, or the bureau have control over it all. I don't want either of those outcomes."

Kip shook his head. "We're not using Elba as bait. End of."

"We don't have a fucking choice," Hem growled. "We'll make sure nothing happens to her. I swear on my life, the bureau will not get her."

"You can't guarantee that," Kip said. "It's too dangerous."

"Staying here in this room is dangerous," Elba said, drawing their fiery gazes from each other. "I think it's a good plan."

Kip swore under his breath and turned away, magic pulsing on his skin.

Hem stared at him for a moment before turning to Lindsey and Lawrence. "Do you have somewhere to aim for? Is there a safe location somewhere?"

Lawrence pulled a small piece of paper from his jeans and waved his fingers across its surface.

Hem pulled his square of magic paper from his pocket and nodded at whatever he saw there.

"What exactly do you plan on doing?" Lindsey asked, her power swirling in wreathes around her legs and torso.

"Best you don't know," Kip said, rolling up his sleeves. "Plausible deniability and all that."

Lawrence slid his mobile into his pocket and flexed his fingers, sparkles glistening along his arms. "I've told the guards outside to let you past and then to escort us to the right. One of them, Jag, he'll go with you and show you the best way out in the opposite direction. We should be able to make it to the—"

"Plausible deniability," Hem cut him off.

Elba's entire body was trembling. Whether it was with fear or nerves or a combination of both, she wasn't sure. On the other side of the door, the bangs and screams grew louder.

She was sure she could smell smoke. Kip stepped closer, his magic lessening as he placed his hands on her shoulders.

"Breathe." Leaning closer, he whispered against her ear. "We're going to leave here and turn left. Stay close. We're going to move through like a battering ram. Element of surprise. Keep your magic up and blast anyone that comes close to you. I don't care if it's bureau or freedom, okay?"

He pulled back to search her eyes, frowning at the tremble that shook her where she stood. "Do you trust us?"

Elba drew in a slow, shaky breath. "Yes."

"I won't leave your side, okay?" Kip said, his hands sliding down her arms.

Hem touched her elbow, a grim smile on his face. "Ready?"

As Elba nodded her response, Hem's black smoke ripped from his hands as Kip's gold flecked silver flames roared to life at his fingers. Trying to block out the yells of terror and pain echoing along the corridor, she stared at her hands. She'd enjoyed commanding the magic forward, but now, knowing it could kill Kipling, she was frozen with fear.

Before, she hadn't known she could syphon his power. After all, it was a small amount of magic needed to tie someone to a chair. Now, facing whatever lay on the other side of the doors, Elba knew it would be a much greater pull on his magic. She lowered her trembling hands, but before she could speak, Hem waved a hand, and the doors flew open.

"Let's do this."

TWENTY

WHATEVER ELBA WAS EXPECTING as she ran after Hem into the hallway, it wasn't what awaited her. Her breath caught in her throat as she slammed into a wall of smoke and sparks, the screaming and grunting so much louder now. One of the guards, a tall, dark-eyed man wearing a royal blue turban, turned to them as they emerged.

"Jag?" Hem asked, surveying the clouded corridor.

The man gave a brief nod before motioning for them to follow. Elba stared as he and Hem were instantly swallowed by the dark mist. Kip nudged her forward, slicing a path through the dense smoke with his magic.

The corridor seemed shorter than before and, as the cries grew louder, Elba found herself tripping over crumpled figures lining the walls. She didn't let her gaze linger to see which side they were from.

It was only when the smoke thinned, revealing an enormous open space, that Elba realised they'd come a different way than before, bypassing the control room altogether. They paused for the first time, the blasts of magic zigzagging across the room blazing against the shields being expended to deflect them. The air was thick with the smell of magic and she realised that the piles of material she'd noticed scattered around the space were bodies. Elba staggered backwards until she found Kip's solid form behind her. It was as though an entire floor of the building sprawled out before them, nothing but windows and pillars dotted around the enormous space.

"What is this place?" she breathed.

"Training space," Jag replied, his eyes darting over the mayhem, trying to find a path through.

Elba froze as a woman in a suit sprinted across the room, blood pouring from her forehead and purple flames so dark, they almost looked black, tearing from her hands. She threw her hand forward with such force it sounded like a gunshot as the magic bounded from her toward a cluster of Freedoms.

The Freedoms pulled up shields of their own magic, deflecting the strike, but not as easily as they should have. Elba frowned as she surveyed the damage. The Freedoms were twice as powerful as the bureau. Even though the numbers on each side seemed fairly even, they weren't winning. Something was wrong.

"That's the way out," Jag called over his shoulder, pointing at a set of double doors at the far end of the space. "Get to those doors and then use the stairs. Go down to the third floor and then through the fire escape. You can magic from there. It's a sort of escape hatch in the wards."

Before they could question him further, he launched himself into the fray, shooting a spear of orange light at a suited man blasting a Freedom into a corner. The man ignited instantly, his scream rippling through the flames as his black suit turned orange. A whimper escaped Elba's mouth and Kip's hand closed around hers.

"Come on," Hem said, his voice tight. "Let's get out of here."

They'd barely made it a step when a cry rang out. Elba froze as a cluster of suited Men turned to her, their eyes blazing. Bennet stood amongst them, no sign of the burns on his face from the flames she'd unleashed upon him.

"Get her," he snarled.

Kip's hand tightened around hers as he pulled her forward, launching into a sprint across the room. Hem sent blasts of power out to the sides, sending those who tried to stop them crashing to the floor. They made it halfway across the room before someone slammed into Kip, causing him to stagger, his grip on her hand breaking. Elba fell to the floor with a thud, the air whooshing from her lungs.

Kip righted himself effortlessly, engaging his attacker in hand-to-hand combat as Hem prevented others from joining in. Elba scrambled to her feet, her eyes frantically darting between them as she watched, helpless. Her fingers twitched at her side, but she refused to call on her magic. Her heart dropped to her stomach as she pictured his pained face in the boardroom. She couldn't risk hurting him again.

A low moan near Elba's feet pulled her from her thoughts. Glancing down, she found a Freedom sprawled at the base of a pillar, blood coating half of her face. It took Elba a moment to realise that her legs were trapped under a pile of three other bodies. They weren't moving.

"Help," the woman rasped.

Elba looked between the trapped woman and where Hem and Kip were fending off the Men. Before she could question whether it was a good idea, she reached down and took hold of the woman's hands, pulling her from underneath the bodies. She gritted her teeth, her shoulders and knees protesting as she heaved with all her might. The Freedom roared with pain as Elba pulled her free.

Breathing hard, she pushed herself to sitting, leaning against the pillar. "Thank you," she panted.

"Come on!"

Elba blinked as Kip grabbed hold of her wrist and pulled. The man he'd been fighting lay in a bloodied heap and she hopped over him as they resumed their sprint to the door. Elba chanced a glance over her shoulder just in time to see the Freedom she'd helped mutter a healing spell—a shimmer of magic coating her body.

A deafening boom caused the room to shudder and a cloud of white plumed toward them. Kip skidded to a halt, tugging her behind a pillar, Hem just behind. They stood, backs pressed against the concrete, chests rising and falling.

"Why aren't the Freedoms owning this?" Hem wheezed. "They're so much stronger."

Kip peered around the pillar, one arm pinning Elba to his side. "I have no idea. The Men still have restrictors in. Their magic is at like, twenty-five percent."

Elba swallowed, bile rising in her throat as the wet sounds of blood and sliced flesh punctuated the air between the booms and crashes of magic. With the wards preventing both sides from being able to magic, a lot of the combat was hand to hand, and it was the most brutal thing she'd ever witnessed.

"Are you okay?" Kip said, pressing a kiss to the top of her head.

Elba tried to nod but trembled instead.

"We're more than halfway," Hem said, glancing around the corner. "Summon your magic, Elba. Don't think I haven't noticed you haven't used it yet. These fuckers won't think twice about using theirs on you, so act first, think later. Okay?"

She nodded, but holding her hands out in front of her, she still couldn't bring herself to command the flames to her fingers. Kip traced his fingers along her palm before tipping her chin to look up at him.

"You won't hurt me," he said, moving his head to hold her gaze even as she tried to look away. "You've commanded your magic dozens of times without draining me. Trust yourself."

Elba forced herself to look in his eyes. He'd referred to it as her magic again. As much as a part of her wanted it to be, she knew it wasn't. It was borrowed. Stolen. A body smashed into the other side of the pillar and she winced. Kip gave her an encouraging smile and taking a deep breath, she commanded the flames to her fingers.

The feeling was tinged with fear rather than exhilaration and she decided that if they got out of there, she'd never call on his magic again. They'd find a way to get the conduit scar off her skin and she could go back to being normal. Normal.

"Let's go," Hem commanded, black smoke tinging the flames that rippled at his fingers as he stepped out from behind the pillar. With Kip's hand at the small of her back, Elba took a breath and followed.

Magic hung suspended in the air, in puffs of cloud, dust and sparks of every colour of the rainbow. It filled her lungs and stung her eyes as she wafted her way through, her flames burning brighter through certain patches and clearing the way in others. It was only as she stepped out of a thick patch of turquoise mist, that she realised she must have slowed. Kip and Hem were a few meters ahead, blasting magic at a group of suited Men Elba didn't recognise. A shiver ran down her spine as she realised Bennet was probably out there some-where, looking for her.

"Elba?"

She whirled at the vaguely familiar voice and found the woman who'd tried to claim Kipling at the bureau slumped against a pillar, blood splattered across her face.

"Bryony?" The name came to her and she glanced back in Kip and Hem's direction. "Are you okay?"

The woman snorted, the sound wetter than it should have been. "Do I look okay?"

Turning to Kip and Hem once more, Elba took a step away. Bryony was the enemy. The bureau was the enemy.

"I'm sorry I was a dick," she rasped. "Back at the bureau."

Elba took another step away. "Whatever. It's fine."

"If I'd known you would be leaving me to die a couple of days later," she chuckled, "I'd have been nicer to you."

Elba sucked in a breath. Was she dying? She couldn't tell where she was injured. Everyone seemed to be coated in blood. So much blood.

"Look, I'm too injured to fight," Bryony reasoned. "If you could just help me to my feet, I might be able to get out of here alive."

She was the enemy. Elba stared. Could she just leave her to die? Her eyes flitted to Bryony's long legs and the smart black pumps on her slender feet. Was the restrictor there as it had been with Kip and Hem? The Men didn't know. They didn't know that the people they served were working against them. They were as blind as Kip and Hem had been. Elba closed her eyes for a second, nausea rocking through her as she realised Kip would have been in situations like this before—fighting for the bureau.

Opening her eyes, she studied Bryony again. It wasn't her fault. With one last glance at Kip and Hem, she stepped to the slumped brunette and held out her hand. Even before Bryony stood, even before she wrapped an arm around her throat, Elba saw the glint of triumph in her golden eyes. It was a trap.

TWENTY-ONE

ELBA GASPED for air as Bryony's arm clamped tighter around her windpipe, her other hand wielding beautiful emerald flames, which she held close enough to her face to cause her to flinch.

"Go on," she hissed in her ear. "Call for help."

Elba struggled against her grasp, trying to summon flames to burn or push Bryony away, but it was like throwing a match at a brick wall.

"Don't bother," Bryony said. "Your magic won't work on me."

Elba tried to ask why, but the word was nothing more than a strangled gasp. She clawed at the arm pressed against her throat, her feet struggling to stay balanced as she searched for Kipling. She found him just as he knocked a man to the ground.

It was agony watching him as he turned, shaking out his hand, concern creasing his brow as he realised, she wasn't there. Seeing it turn to panic as he looked for her. The panic then melting into terror as he found her pressed up against Bryony's tall, lean body, struggling for air, before finally settling into pure white-hot rage.

"Let her go," he ground out, his silver eyes flaring with the promise of violence as he strode towards them.

Bryony chuckled at Elba's ear. "So protective. Is she still flavour of the week?"

"Let her go, Bry, and maybe we let you out of here unharmed," Hem said, stepping to Kip's side.

Elba noted the hand slightly in front of Kip, black smoke curling, as though preparing to hold him back if need be.

"I don't think so." Bryony squeezed Elba's throat tighter and her eyes rolled at the lack of oxygen. "This whole situation is ridiculous. You two should be the ones bringing her in but instead, you're here with the enemy. I couldn't believe it when I heard you'd been turned."

Hem took a small step forward. "You have no idea. They're not the enemy you think they are."

"Seriously?" Bryony snorted. "You're brainwashed. Just like Selena. I can't believe they managed to turn both of you. I honestly thought you were smarter than that."

Elba blinked, trying to focus as the edges of her vision darkened. They wouldn't tell her. They couldn't. It wasn't likely she'd believe them about the restrictors or the Grand Wizard, and if she reported back to the First Tier, letting the bureau know the Freedoms knew what they were up to . . . It wasn't worth the risk.

Kip hadn't taken his eyes off her for a second and Elba knew what he was trying to tell her. He wanted her to use her power. She'd have to show them, if only to give it one last try. Gasping for air, she called on his power. Her fingers flickered with silver flame that spluttered out as soon as it formed.

"Stop trying to use your magic," Bryony snapped. "You're not strong enough. You'd need to be a supernova to blast through the dampeners."

Was that why the Freedoms weren't winning so easily? Elba couldn't begin to imagine how the bureau was dampening the immense power of the Freedoms. Wards. Artefacts? Whatever it was, it was effective to say the least.

Bryony squeezed her arm against her neck and Elba sagged against her. Kip strode forward, Hem reaching too late to grab for his arm.

"She can't breathe! Let go of her right now." Kip raised an arm covered in flames, but Bryony just laughed.

"Blast me, you blast her." She leaned her head, surveying Elba with golden eyes. "She's a pretty little thing. Did you run out of people to fuck at the bureau?"

Kip's jaw tightened, his glare fixing on Bryony. "I'm not going to ask you again. Let her go."

"Don't go thinking you're special," she cooed, pressing her cheek against hers. "You're just the latest in a long line of soulless fucks as he tries to fill the damaged void inside that pretty shell."

"Shut your mouth, Bryony," Hem barked, grabbing a fist of Kipling's sweater as he tried to hold him back.

She brought her mouth closer to Elba's ear. "Did he fuck you over his desk yet?"

Kip's eyes widened ever so slightly but he kept his gaze fixed on Bryony, his flames flaring, and his jaw clenched.

"That's his signature move," she drawled. "He does the brooding dark, mysterious thing so well doesn't he?"

Elba's stomach clenched but she tried to balance herself, to push back against Bryony. Her magic wouldn't work, but if she could somehow knock her over.

Bryony smiled, almost purring against her neck. "And that thing he does with his tongue—"

"Green is an ugly colour on you, Bry," Hem spat. "Let Elba go."

Bryony snorted. "Is she really worth it? Is she that good of a lay that you'd work with the enemy and throw away everything you've worked toward your entire lives?"

"You have no idea what you're talking about." There was a calmness to Kip's voice that made Elba blink.

It was then that she felt it—a pulse along the invisible thread linking her to his magic. Elba gasped as power flooded through into her core, filling her with crackling flames.

Bryony tensed at her back, her emerald magic flaring. "What's happening?"

Silver flame lapped beneath her skin, her lungs expanding as she began to glow with power. Kip gave her a small smile as he paled before her, staggering backwards. Hem whipped his gaze between them, understanding flashing in his navy eyes.

"What the fuck are you doing?" he shouted, grabbing hold of Kip's arm as he doubled over in pain.

His power exploded through her like a burst pipe, but panic blazed in Elba's chest as he fell to his knees. "Stop it, Kip," she pleaded.

Bryony held Elba tighter, but the flames roared, trying to break free—the magic pushing to release from where it was building pressure inside her. Bryony had told Elba she would need to be a supernova to break free and that's exactly what Kip was turning her into. Tears filled Elba's eyes and she blinked them back.

Hem stared between them, his eyes wide. "Use the magic, Elba," he shouted. "Blast the bitch. It's the only way we can make him stop."

Elba wrenched Bryony's hand from her throat, drawing a yelp of surprise from her. Gulping down air, she summoned the power around her, pushing it out in a blast of blinding white light so bright she had to close her eyes. Bryony flew backwards, slamming against a pillar before sliding to the ground.

Elba didn't wait to see if she got back up, instead, falling to her knees at Kip's side. Collapsed in a heap, his lips blue, she stared up at Hem only to find her own terror-stricken expression reflected. She grasped Kip's hand, trying to send the remnants of magic still fluttering in her chest back down the string connecting them. It was nothing compared with what he'd sent through to her. Mere drops. Swiping at the hot tears blurring her vision, she hoped against hope it was enough.

Around them, the fighting seemed to have paused. It was all because of her, she realised. Not just pausing because of her blinding explosion, but because of what the conduit stone had made her. She was the reason the bureau was here—the reason so many people were lying on the ground around her, dead or injured. It was almost laughable. She was a no one. A chance Normal in the wrong place at the wrong time.

Drawing a shaky breath, Elba glanced at the people standing around the room staring in awestruck silence. One pair of narrowed brown eyes glared at her. She swallowed, taking in Bennet—Jay at his side—their magic roiling at their wrists and their eyes gleaming with challenge.

"Did you burn yourself out, love?" Bennet asked, those hot, red sparks crackling at his fingertips.

"Shit," Hem muttered. "Shit."

Elba pressed her hand against Kip's chest, the faint beat of his heart her only tether as she looked across the room at the doors they needed to get to. It was too far. They'd never make it. Surely there was another way to get out and evade the wards sealing in the building. There had to be.

Bennet strode towards them, Jay at his side swathed in his green mist. Hem stood, summoning his own magic, but before the Men could get close, Jag and several other Freedoms dived at them, filling the air with plumes of power once more.

Under the cover of shouts and yells filling the air, Hem dragged Kip up from the ground. He slung an arm over his shoulder, grunting under the weight while Elba tried to hold him up on the other side.

"Let's go," he hissed.

They managed about three meters before they were forced to take refuge behind a pillar.

"We'll never make it. It's too far with Kip like this." Elba stared up at his pallid face, his dark lashes brushing his cheeks. "Is he going to be okay?"

Hem didn't answer, instead pressing his lips together before looking away, surveying the fighting around them. "Fuck. Fuck."

"Is there another door do you think?" Elba mused, her heart thudding with such force it rocked her body as she stood. "Or an air conditioning vent? Something. Anything?"

"Elba," Hem said carefully. "I have an idea, but you're not going to like it."

She turned to him, fear lacing her spine at what she saw in his eyes.

"We're going to run for that window in front of us," he explained, motioning with his head, "and jump."

Elba recoiled. "Excuse me?"

"Look, I don't want to jump out of a window any more than you do. Believe me, I'm open to other suggestions."

She shook her head. They'd fall to their deaths. Even as she opened her mouth to protest, her eyes widened as she realised what he was suggesting. As soon as they were outside the building, they could magic to safety. Even if it meant magicking in mid-air.

"Can you magic all three of us?" she breathed, trying not to think what would happen if he couldn't.

"I'll have to."

Elba blinked. "That doesn't fill me with confidence."

"Do you have any magic left?" Hem asked, staring not at her chest, but at the glowing mark hidden beneath her sweater.

She swallowed, eyeing Kip's limp figure. "I . . . I don't know."

"You don't need to take any of his," Hem reassured her. "Just what you have inside you. Is there anything left?"

Elba focused, trying to command whatever dregs of magic were still underneath her skin to appear. Flame flickered at her fingertips and she filled with shame. She'd tried to send it all back to Kip. It clearly hadn't worked.

"I need you to blast the window out," Hem instructed. "It's going to take all my strength to get him up and out and it's not going to be graceful. If you can get rid of the glass, before we get there, we stand a better chance."

Elba nodded. "I'll try."

"You're not filling me with confidence," Hem said, his eyes sparkling.

Before she could retort, Hem pulled his magic around them, shrouding them in a fine black mist, before pushing Elba toward the window. She pulled at her power, Hem breaking into a limping jog beside her with Kip draped over his side. Holding out her hands, she sent a blast of white-hot flame at the glass, commanding it to shatter, melt, disappear —whatever it needed to do to vanish.

There was barely time to see whether it worked before they reached the low sill, Hem grabbing her arm and pulling her over the edge as they toppled out into the cool air, plummeting toward the pavement far below.

Elba didn't have the chance to draw breath to scream before black smoke swallowed her.

TWENTY-TWO

WHEN SOLID GROUND materialised beneath her, Elba's knees buckled and she collapsed to the floor, vomiting on the plush grey carpet. *Carpet?* She braced herself on her hands, swallowing.

"It's okay," a familiar voice said as a hand gave her shoulder a comforting pat. "You're safe now."

Elba looked up to find Lawrence crouched beside her, a queasy expression on his face. "Oh my god. I'm so sorry about the carpet."

"It's fine," he said. Lifting a hand, the vomit disappeared leaving only the faintest odour lingering in the air. "Be careful with him."

It took her a second to realise Lawrence wasn't talking to her. Still trying to get her bearings, she turned to find Kip being hoisted onto a stretcher, Hem standing over him, tensed. She tried to get to her feet, to follow as they carried Kip away, but Lawrence kept hold of her arm.

"They'll look after him," he said gently. "Why don't you and Hemingway get cleaned up and then someone will take you to him?"

Elba frowned, looking down at herself for the first

time. She couldn't contain the gasp as she saw the singe marks and tears in her clothes—the splatters of blood. Blinking, she looked at Hem. He was in an even worse state, his thigh bleeding through a slash in his jeans and the right sleeve of his sweater half torn from the shoulder.

"Ada will show you to your rooms," Lawrence said as a petite Asian woman stepped forward, sympathy shining in her dark eyes.

Elba gave her a half smile before looking past her, taking in the room. They were in what looked like the reception for a spa. Relaxing music played softly from somewhere, the walls adorned with artistic pictures of pebbles and water. The man behind the desk wore a white tunic as he tapped at a computer.

"Where are we?" Elba asked, gaping at the fountain adorning an entire wall, the water trickling down polished granite.

"This is our back up headquarters," Lawrence explained, his face grim. "Only a handful of people know of its existence."

Ada reached out and placed a hand on Elba's shoulder. "Come on, let me take you to freshen up."

Exhaustion stealing any coherent thought from her lips, she nodded. Hem draped an arm around her shoulders, pulling her into a side hug and they followed Ada through an entrance half concealed by a thin gauzy material.

The corridor had a series of long, narrow windows along its length and Elba glanced out, squinting at the scenery. They definitely weren't in the city anymore. Tall trees lined the border of sprawling gardens, with what looked like mountains in the distance. She frowned. That couldn't be right, surely?

"Here you go," Ada said, coming to a halt. "Your rooms are across the hall from each other. Here are your key cards. If you need anything, just dial 'one' from the telephone in the room."

Elba took the pearlescent key card from her and stared at it until Hem reached out and took it from her, swiping it against the panel.

"I've got her," he said.

Elba blinked. Was he talking about her? Hem placed his hands on her shoulders and guided her into the room, closing the door behind them.

"You're in shock," he said gently, moving to stand in front of her. "That whole thing was pretty intense. It's one of the biggest battles I've been in for sure."

She blinked again, staring up at him. "Kip . . ."

"He'll be okay," Hem said, although his eyes flickered with uncertainty. "I'm fairly sure they'll have good doctors here."

Elba nodded and stepped away to the window, the echoes of screams still ringing in her ears. How many people had died in that room, that building, today? How many people were injured right now because of her? She closed her eyes and leaned her head against the window.

"Get cleaned up and we'll go find out where he is," Hem said. "Okay?"

"Okay." She tried to give him a smile, but her face crumpled, tears filling her eyes instead.

Hem stepped forward and crushed her to his chest. "Hey, now. It's okay. We're all okay."

"It's my fault," she choked out against his torn and singed sweater.

"Bollocks." Hem squeezed her tighter, rubbing a large hand up and down her back. "How could it possibly be your fault?"

Elba drew a shaky breath, trying to ignore the smell of smoke lacing his clothes. "If I hadn't used the conduit stone, they wouldn't be chasing us. They're looking for me."

Hem stepped back, holding her at arm's length as he held her gaze. "Like I said, bollocks. Yes, they want the stone, but you have to remember Kip and I lost the stone in the first place. And I think us springing Selena has something to do with why they're after us, too. I read the spell that bound you that first time and I, for one, don't regret it. If I hadn't, Kip would have died."

Elba swiped at her eyes, unconvinced.

"This is the First Tier's fault," Hem continued, pulling her back against his chest. "It's so much bigger than any of us. Don't you dare blame yourself. And as for Kip, that's his own damn fault for trying to be a bloody martyr."

Elba's heart clenched at the thought of Kip collapsing as he tried to give her all his magic and she screwed her eyes closed, gripping Hem tight.

"Right, come on," he said after a moment. "I'm dying for a shower and in a place like this, I bet the showers are incredible."

She smiled and squeezed his hand as he stepped away. "Thank you."

Hem held his hands up as he walked to the door. "Nothing to thank me for, Elba. I'll call for you in fifteen."

She stared at the door long after it had closed, trying to process the events of the day. Maybe Hem was right, but the guilt still lingered. Guilt that was deepened as she remembered Siena. With a groan, she rubbed her hands over her face. How would they explain that they weren't at the hotel anymore?

With a heavy sigh, Elba turned and walked into the bathroom, her mouth falling open as she took in the wet room with a waterfall shower. Switching on the water, she stripped off her torn and dirtied clothes, abandoning them on the floor. The shower had an enormous head, sending what appeared to be scented water cascading down against the pale mother-of-pearl flecked tiles.

As soon as she stepped under the spray, Elba felt her tensed muscles uncoil. An array of soaps lined one of the walls and she selected a lavender scented concoction. Massaging the fragrant suds into her hair, she replayed Hem's words. Kip had been reckless trying to send her all that magic. There would have been another way, she was sure. If he had died, did he not realise the pain and guilt she'd have to live with? Did Kip not understand how much she cared about him? Hem hadn't seemed surprised by his actions, but then he knew how little self-worth he held for himself.

She shook the thought from her head. He wasn't dead. Even though it was fainter than it had ever been, she could still feel the line between them. More like a fine piece of hair than a piece of string, but there, nonetheless.

Rinsing the soap from her hair, Elba's stomach lurched as she recalled Bryony's words. It hadn't been a surprise. She knew Kip's bedroom prowess was not a fluke. It was the result of *a lot* of practice. He knew how to play her body like an instrument—a virtuoso with incredible skill. Even so, she found herself gripping the sponge until her knuckles turned white.

The anger lingered as she towelled herself off and found that it wasn't just Bryony that she wanted to punch in the throat, but Kip himself. A pair of soft pale grey linen trousers and a matching kimono-style top had been laid out on her bed and she wondered whether they had been there the whole time, or someone had put them there while she was in the shower. With people magicking in and out of rooms, it was anyone's guess.

Elba had just hung her towel up, sliding her feet into the soft slippers beside the bed, when Hem knocked.

"Do you feel better?" he asked as she opened the door.

Wearing the same clothes as her, the material stretched over his biceps and the vee of the wrap around top exposing the top of his muscled chest, Hem's blond hair was tied back, still dark from the water. His eyes gave her a once over, as though checking she was all in one piece. She wasn't sure she was.

"The shower was incredible," she replied, dodging the question.

Hem groaned, throwing his head back. "It was beyond incredible. I want to marry that shower and have little shower babies with it."

Elba laughed and stepped out into the hallway. "That's all kinds of disturbing."

She noticed his limp as they walked down the hallway, but bit back the question. He'd have used magic to heal it, but she knew larger wounds took time.

The young man at the reception desk looked up as they entered the foyer, a bright smile lighting his hazel eyes. "Are you feeling better?"

"Much better, thanks," Hem said, leaning on the desk. "Can you tell us where they took our friend?"

He nodded, picking up a phone. "I'll just find out for you."

Elba turned and looked at the room, wondering again where they were. How far had Hem magicked them? How far was it possible to travel by magic? As if punctuating her thoughts, Ada appeared in the middle of the foyer in a plume of white mist.

"Come with me," she said, giving them a brief look over before leading them through a different doorway.

Elba swallowed her nerves and stepped to her side. "I was wondering if you could give me some advice about something else."

Ada's answering smile undid some of the knots in her stomach. "Of course, how can I help?"

"My cousin is staying at the hotel we were at before the headquarters. I know what the bureau is capable of and I'm worried about her safety." She felt Hem tense a little beside her.

Ada gave a thoughtful frown. "Is she a Magic?"

"No." Elba folded her arms around her middle. "She has no idea."

"This place might be our headquarters but it a real functioning spa, too. Although mostly used by Magics, we have protocols in place for when Normals are in the building. Let me check with Lawrence and we'll see about finding a room for her here. It won't be long term I'm afraid."

"That's fine," she gushed. "I'll happily take a short-term solution, thank you."

Ada inclined her head in reply, then knocked on the door they'd stopped in front of.

A tall willowy man with shoulder length dark hair and a long black tunic opened it, looking at each of them in turn before stepping back to let them in. Elba smiled at him as she walked past, and he dipped his head in response.

"This is Dr. Tanner," Ada said. "He's the best magical healer in the country."

Elba wondered whether he was permanently stationed with the Freedoms or whether he'd been brought in especially. Either way, as her gaze found Kip, deathly still under pale covers in the middle of the darkened room, she was nothing but grateful.

"Is he okay?" she whispered as Hem stepped to his side, frowning as he looked him over.

"He'll live," Dr. Tanner said. "He had a few superficial injuries which are either healed or almost healed, but the lack of magic . . . I've never come across anything like it before."

Elba swallowed. "Is it gone?"

"No. If it was gone, he would have died." He stepped to Kip's side and hovered a hand over the covers, a faint glow emanating from his fingertips. "He had a little magic left, which is what saved his life."

Elba sucked in a breath, her fingers clenching into fists. Was that the magic she'd pushed back into him? "Will it be enough?" she asked. "Does it regenerate? Can I give him more?"

"It will regenerate eventually. How are your own magic levels?" the man eyed her curiously.

"I don't feel any different than usual." She wasn't sure when the empty feeling she'd experienced after Bryony had disappeared. She hadn't tried to feel his magic, but now she was aware of it stroking beneath her skin. "Can I try to give him more?"

The doctor frowned, glancing down at Kip. "I don't think it would hurt. I have to admit that I'm curious about the link between you."

Elba's hand reached for the glowing scar beneath her top. Hem stepped to her side and took hold of her other hand.

"Are you sure you're up to it?" he asked.

"I think so." She concentrated on the skinny hair of power between them and fed the flames through to him. It was like pushing an orange through a straw and she squeezed Hem's hand so hard he sucked in a breath.

"Fascinating," the doctor whispered as Kip drew in a shuddering breath, his eyes moving behind his eyelids.

Elba sagged against Hem as she let go of the link. She had no idea how much she'd passed back, but Dr. Tanner seemed pleased enough.

"Lawrence would like to speak with you," Ada said, dragging her eyes from Kip's sleeping figure.

Elba took a step closer to the bed, giving Hem a pleading look. "Can you go without me?" she asked. "I'd like to stay a little longer."

Hem squeezed her shoulder. "I'm sure that'll be fine."

Ada dipped her head in response. "I'll ask about your cousin, too."

"Thank you." Elba slipped her fingers between Kip's limp digits as Hem followed her into the hallway.

Dr. Tanner paused, his mouth open, as though contemplating saying something. He seemed to think better of it and smiled as he walked to the door. "I'll give you some privacy."

Elba nodded her thanks, breathing a sigh of relief as the quiet enveloped them. She knew he had most likely been wanting to ask about the conduit stone. Probably eager to run some tests. Reaching out, she ran an ebony lock of Kip's hair between her fingers. She'd let them soon. If only to find out more about it herself—whether it was permanent or something that would fade.

Kip frowned, a soft murmur on his lips. Elba stroked his face, soothing whatever was worrying him. A nightmare perhaps? This was the second time in as many weeks she'd almost lost him. Was it skill or just pure damn luck that he'd not died before now? Perhaps she'd have to ask Hem if it was always like this.

"Hey."

Elba jumped as she found Kip's eyes open, watching her. "You're awake."

He blinked. "It would appear so."

She watched, heart pounding as he pushed himself to sitting, the covers falling to his waist revealing his naked torso, flecked with almost healed burns. She exhaled. He was okay. He was really okay.

"I'm not dead, then," he said, a tight smile on his lips.

Anger roared to the surface, painting Elba's cheeks red as she slammed both hands into his chest. "You almost died!"

His eyes widened in shock as he flinched away from her. "But I didn't."

Something that felt like a growl ripped from her throat. "Not for lack of trying, you selfish prick!" She slammed her hands into his chest again.

"Elba—"

"Why would you do that?" she pressed, tears blurring her vision as she balled her hands into fists. "Why would you do something so reckless? There would have been another way . . . You can't just . . . If you'd . . ." She punctuated each thought with a thump to the chest.

Kip grabbed hold of her hands and a sob burst from her lips. "Elba," he soothed. "I'm sorry. I couldn't stand by and let her hurt you. I couldn't see another way."

Elba sniffed, shaking her head. "Killing yourself is never an option. How you can even think that I'd be okay with that —that Hem would be okay with that . . ."

Kip pulled her fists closer, his eyes darkening. "If I ever have to choose between your life and mine, I'll choose yours every time. I'll never apologise for that."

Elba stared at him, anger rippling under her skin, even as her heart ached at his words. "You don't get to do that," she said. "You—"

He leaned forward and stole the words from her lips with a kiss. When he pulled back, she opened her mouth to finish what she was saying but he kissed her again, a small smile pulling at his mouth.

Wrenching her fists from his hands, she stepped back from the bed. "Stop it. I'm still mad at you."

Kip sighed, slumping back against the pillow he'd propped behind him. "I'm not dead. You're not dead. I'm assuming Hem's not dead?"

Elba rolled her eyes.

He tried to reach for her, but she stepped to the side. "What do I have to say to stop you from being angry with me?"

"Last night," she said. "Just last night, you promised you wouldn't leave. You said you weren't planning on putting distance between us. I think death is a pretty big fucking distance."

Kip stared at her, his jaw set, as something that looked like pain flickered in his eyes.

"I want to trust you," she said, her voice barely above a whisper. "But how can I?"

He reached for her again, his fingers brushing her forearm. "Elba . . ."

"Why?" Elba pushed, shaking her head. "You're so much more important. You're . . . What did Lawrence say? The 'best of the best'. I'm just a Normal who keeps getting in the way and fucking everything up."

She hated the words as soon as they left her lips, but there was a kernel of truth hidden under them. Bryony had said she was just the latest conquest and part of her believed it. Why would he choose her when he could have his pick of anyone?

Kip leaned forward and gripped her hand, tugging her towards him as his eyes searched hers. "Why are you talking like that?"

She looked away, fixing her gaze on the soft white sheets.

"Does this have anything to do with what Bryony said?" he said, the words dripping with disgust. "Don't let that bitch get in your head."

"I'm not," she lied. "It's not as if I didn't know there had been others . . ."

Kip sat back, stroking his thumbs across her hands. "You just didn't realise how much of a man whore I was?"

"Oh, I knew you were a man whore." Elba smiled, a blush creeping onto her cheeks. "You and Hem made that perfectly clear from the get-go."

To her amusement, Kip's skin also pinkened. "Good point. She was wrong about you, though. You know that, right?"

Elba returned her gaze to the sheets and he reached up and stroked her cheek.

"You're not like the others," he said. "Elba, I . . ."

Her heartbeat rocked against her ribs as she lifted her eyes to meet his, only to find him staring at her hand, his dark lashes brushing his cheek. When he looked up, her breath caught in her throat at the softness in his gaze.

"I'm falling for you, Elba. I've never let myself get this close to someone before and I know I'm fucking it all up, but I'm trying. I really am." He studied her face, nervousness flickering across his expression. "Are you going to hit me again?"

Elba took his beautiful face in her hands and kissed him.

TWENTY-THREE

THEY'D WON. Not the war, but the battle at least. Hem sprawled out on the large bed in his room, arms behind his head as he filled Elba and Kip in on his meeting with Lawrence. After receiving word from the headquarters, it turned out that most of the Men had fled not long after Hem had pulled them through the window.

"They managed to capture a handful for questioning, though," Hem said. "It's hard to know how to feel about that."

"Is Bryony one of them?" Kip asked, his eyes blazing. "Because I know how I'd feel about that."

Hem snorted. "She deserves everything she gets."

A shiver ran down Elba's spine as images of Selena's interrogation flashed in her mind. "Did they figure out how they got in?"

"Lawrence and his team have their suspicions," Hem said. "He thinks they've managed to syphon off enough magic from the GW to supercharge artefacts."

Kip blew out a long breath. "We're running out of time, aren't we?"

The heavy silence was interrupted by a knock on the door. Hem slid off the bed to answer it with a shrug.

Ada gave a small nod as he opened the door. "Just to let you know that you're good to bring your cousin. Just let us know how you'd like to proceed. We can send a car if you'd like."

"Thank you." Elba stood, giving the petite woman a smile. "I think I'll go and get her. I still need to figure out my story. Do we just bring her to the reception and check her in?"

Ada gave another nod. "Absolutely. We'll be expecting her."

"Thank you." Elba exhaled as Ada turned and left, resting her head in her hands. "How do I even do this?"

"Well, you're not going to go and get her by yourself, that's for damn sure," Hem said. "All three of us are going."

"What do I tell her, though?" Elba groaned. "How do I explain?"

"Maybe you tell her the truth," Kip suggested.

Hem barked a laugh. "Hilarious."

"I'm serious." Kip turned to Elba. "Why don't we go speak to her and take it from there."

Hem folded his arms across his chest. "I suppose, if all else fails, we can erase her memory."

"Don't you dare." Elba gasped.

Kip stood and held out his hand for her. "Come on. No time like the present."

Elba stared at his hand. "Are you strong enough to magic?"

"Perhaps I should take you both," Hem suggested. He held up his hand as Kip began to protest. "Do you know what happens if you run out of magic halfway through?"

Kip stared at him. "No. Do you?"

"No. But I'm pretty sure you don't want to find out." He held out his hand with a wink. "Come on."

Elba grinned as Kip rolled his eyes and gripped his hand.

"Wait," she said. "What if she's not there?"

Hem shrugged. "Then we try again later. At least we don't have to worry about walking in on her shagging someone now she has her own room."

Kip snorted. "You fucking loved that."

Hem waggled his eyebrows as his black smoke encircled them, stealing the ground from beneath their feet.

As the small hotel room materialised around them, the smoke clearing, Elba yelped in surprise as she found Siena rooting through the drawers in the dresser.

"Shit." Hem hissed.

Siena stood, straightening her suit. "I was wondering when you'd be back."

Elba stared at her, blinking.

Hem sighed. "Well, now we definitely have to erase her memory."

"Try to erase my memory," Siena hissed, "and I'll magic your balls to your forehead."

Elba's head spun. "Excuse me?"

Siena sat down on the bed and crossed one golden leg over the other. "Imagine my surprise, dearest *cugina*, when I arrive at my new office only to find pictures of you, your boyfriend and this one, all over the damn place. What have you got yourself into, Elba?"

Elba felt her knees buckle and Kip slipped a hand around her waist.

"You work for the bureau," he said.

Siena tilted her head in response. "And so did you, until not so long ago, it seems."

"How?" Elba croaked.

Pity filled Siena's eyes and she reached a hand to her. Kip's hand tightened around her waist, warning.

"I didn't turn you in, if that's what you're worried about," she said. "I wanted to find out your side of the story."

"Do they know you're related?" Kip asked. "Because if they do—"

"They have no idea we're related," Siena said. "My job is finding and hiding information. I'm very, very good at it."

"How?" Elba repeated. "How are you a Magic?"

Siena sighed, folding her hands in her lap. "It was our grandmother, Carmella. Our mother's mother. It seems it skipped a generation. Although from what I saw at the bureau, I'm not the only one with magic now."

Elba pressed her fingers to her temples. "I can't . . ."

"Sit down," Siena said, gesturing to the chair by the dresser. "Let me start from the beginning."

Elba stared. All their lives. The holidays they'd spent together. The nights out they'd had, both in London and in Italy. She'd had magic. Had hidden it from her. If Elba hadn't discovered magic in that alley with Kip and Hem, she'd still be hiding it. Siena would be staying at her apartment, working at the Men of Magic headquarters and she'd have been completely oblivious.

"How do we know you haven't already called the bureau?" Hem said, his eyes narrowed.

Siena held his gaze, unflinching. "You don't. I give you my word though. I'd never put Elba in danger. I was in here looking for a way to contact you, to try and find out what's going on."

Hem leaned against the dresser, his arms folded across his chest as Kip eased Elba down into the chair, resting his hands on her shoulders. The squeeze of his fingers did nothing to calm the myriad of emotions swirling in her gut.

"Tell me," Elba murmured.

"My magic appeared when I was eleven," Siena said. She lifted a hand and what sounded like a rumble of thunder sounded, accompanied by tiny diamond-like sparks in a translucent cloud around her fingers. "Luckily, my mother knew about her mother's magic, so she took me to her. She helped me learn how to control it. I wasn't interested in joining the Men, or *gli Uomini* as we say in Italy, and as you know, went to university and got my degree in computer science and programming. I was head hunted before my final year by the Men to work in their cybersecurity section. I was promoted to the head of the department after two years."

"Wait a minute." Hem reached out and poked Kip's arm, his eyes fixed on Siena. "Show us your magic again."

Elba looked up at him, trying to fathom the look of excitement and awe on his face. What did Siena's magic have to do with her promotion? At least she hadn't lied about working with computers. She huffed to herself.

Something flickered across Siena's features as, almost reluctantly, she pulled forth her power. Stronger this time, the sound of thunder was unmistakeable as the shining sparks glistened in the air around her.

"Diamond Thunder!" Hem exclaimed, slapping Kip's arm.

Kip brushed him off, turning his attention back to Siena. "Are you?"

In answer, Siena gave a half shrug, a hint of pride in her small smile.

"What the fuck is 'diamond thunder'?" Elba asked, glaring between her cousin and Hem as she tried and failed to subdue the anger of betrayal.

"Diamond Thunder is a code name," Hem exclaimed, his eyes wide. "The most prolific hacker in the magical world. It never occurred to me that Diamond Thunder would be—"

"A woman?" Siena snapped, folding her arms.

Hem raised his eyebrows. "No. Hot."

"You're a hacker." Elba pressed her fingers to her temples.

"Hacker. Programmer. Security. There's a lot of areas I deal with." Siena leaned forward, trying to catch her eye. "The British Men asked me to come and work for them. Even though I work between all the world's agencies, they said they wanted me to work on something specific and needed me here."

"I can only begin to imagine what they want you to work on." Hem snorted.

Siena ignored him. "Now you know," she said to Elba. "Tell me what's going on. Please?"

Elba lifted her gaze to hers and tried to see the cousin who had always been like a sister to her. She shook her head. "I ran into Kip and Hem when they were trying to stop the Freedoms from getting hold of a conduit stone. Long story short, I found out about magic and we've since discovered that the bureau are evil lying bastards."

"Pretty apt summary," Hem agreed.

Siena blew out a breath. "What do you believe the bureau have done? Because I can access every record they have and then some. Even the ones they think I can't. The bureau has no secrets as far as I can see."

"Then I would be very concerned for your safety," Kip said, his fingers pausing in their rubbing of Elba's shoulders.

"They put restrictors in people," Elba said. "Kip and Hem have removed theirs, but other than the First Tier, all the Men have them."

"Restrictors?" Siena echoed, the word rolling with her accent.

"They kept our powers at about twenty-five percent," Kip seethed. "Do you know if the Italian Men are using them?"

Siena blinked and shook her head, her long dark locks sliding over her shoulders. "I don't think so."

"What does your 'full power' look like?" Kip asked.

In answer, a deafening boom of thunder shook the room, bright sparks suspending in the air before falling to the ground and blinking out.

Elba gawked, a hand over her heart and another clutching Kip's arm.

"So. Cool," Hem murmured.

Kip chuckled. "Yeah, I don't think you have a restrictor."

"Is that it?" Siena asked, her dark brown eyes narrowing. "They're muzzling their dogs?"

"No." Elba looked up at Hem and Kip. "I think you should tell her."

Kip rolled his shoulders and perched on the arm of Elba's chair. "Pearson and the rest of the First Tier have kidnapped the Grand Wizard. They want to drain or distribute his power. We're not sure on that part yet."

"*Mio Dio,*" Siena pressed a hand to her chest. "Are you sure?"

Kip shared a look with Hem. "The leader of the Freedoms is the GW's daughter. The bureau has been feeding the Men fake propaganda to paint them as the enemy for the last few years."

"I need my computer," Siena said.

Before they could utter a word, thunder shook the room and she vanished.

"Shit," Hem hissed. "If she's gone back to the bureau, we're all fucked."

"Calm your tits," Kip said. "I think she believes us. She'll be back in a minute."

Despite the confidence in his tone, Elba felt the tension in the hand resting on her arm. Siena had magic. She worked for the bureau. She was a famed hacker. This was harder to accept than anything else that had happened over the last fortnight. Had she really never noticed the magic? Elba racked her brain, trying to think of any times she'd heard thunder when there hadn't been a storm or seen sparkles out the corner of her eye.

Of course, Siena wouldn't have used magic around her, but . . .

Was that why she'd been having sex with the receptionist? Relieving her magical build up? Her cousin had always been very sexually confident, but perhaps it was more than that.

She'd said it had been a long flight, but did she mean a long flight without using magic? Elba shook her head in silent disbelief.

When the clap of thunder shuddered through the room again, Siena was already tapping away on her laptop, a pair of designer black-rimmed glasses on her nose.

Hem drew a breath and she held up her hand, halting whatever remark he had been about to make. Elba pressed her lips together to stifle her laugh.

"What are you looking for?" Kip asked.

Siena didn't take her eyes from the screen. "Restrictors. I don't need to find everything right now, but if I can find proof of the restrictors, then I will believe everything else you've said."

Reaching up, Elba covered Kip's hand with her own. "And if you believe us?"

Siena paused in her typing, holding Elba's gaze. "Then I'll help however I can. The bureau really wants you, *cugina*."

Elba swallowed. "Yeah. The Freedoms seem to think I could be used as a human conduit stone."

"Excuse me?" Siena sat back, pushing her glasses further up her nose.

Elba summoned silver flames to her right hand, while tugging down her top to expose the top of the glowing scar with the other.

Siena blinked, but said nothing before returning to her laptop, her typing a little more determined.

After a few minutes, she sat back and removed her glasses, pinching the bridge of her nose. "You were just children," she muttered.

Kip tensed. "You found it?"

She nodded. "It's right there in the restricted section of your record."

"What now, then?" he asked. "Will you come with us?"

Siena slid off the bed and crouched in front of Elba,

placing her hands on her knees. "It's up to you. I know you're hurt and angry. I can see it in your face. If you want, I can go back home and lay low."

"No." Elba shook her head, reaching for her cousin's hands. "It's going to take me a while to get my head around it, but I want you to stay. I think you could be a real help to the Freedoms."

Siena smiled. "This isn't the reunion I thought we'd be having."

"Me either." Elba returned the smile. "I'm glad 'Diamond Thunder' is on our side, though."

Her cousin threw back her head in a throaty laugh. "I did not choose the name."

"You'd better grab your stuff." Elba squeezed her hands. "We should get back before the bureau find us."

The laughter drained from Siena's face and she glanced up at Kip. "Yes. We should leave. There's more I need to tell you."

Elba turned to look at Kip as her cousin vanished with a rumble. "What do you think it is?"

Kip's jaw was set as he shook his head. "Something on my record, I suppose. Whatever it is, it doesn't seem like good news."

Elba stood and wrapped her arms around his neck. "Whatever it is, I'm here for you. Okay?"

He nodded, pressing a soft kiss to her lips.

"Diamond fucking Thunder," Hem murmured. "Your cousin is Diamond Thunder."

Kip shook his head. "If I was Pearson, I'd be very, very scared."

Glancing at the laptop sitting, screen dark, on the bed, her cousin's glasses abandoned at its side, Elba couldn't help but agree.

ALSO BY ADDISON ARROWDELL

In the Franklin West Universe:

Stolen

Hidden

Golden (Coming Summer 2022)

If you like witty paranormal romance, check out the rest of her Men of Magic Series:

Freedom & Desire (Men of Magic Book Three)

If you like steamy contemporary reverse harems/poly romance, check out:

Road Trip

ACKNOWLEDGMENTS

You might be interested to know that Hemingway and Kipling came to me in a dream. I have no idea what the dream was about but I loved the idea of a magical crime-fighting duo with those names.

Thank you to my friend GR who supplied the name, Elba. I hope you love her!

Thank you to you, the reader, for getting this far. I hope you continue the journey to find out how everything works out.

Thank you, as always, to my Romance Crew street team for your ongoing support and enthusiasm. You are seriously the best.

ABOUT THE AUTHOR

Addison Arrowdell writes spicy, adult romantic fiction. She believes that even the darkest story should have laugh out loud moments and loves writing witty dialogue.

Want to find out how the story ends?
Freedom & Desire (Men of Magic Book Three)

Subscribe for all the latest news, gossip, giveaways and more!

www.AddisonArrowdell.com

CPSIA information can be obtained
at www.ICGtesting.com
Printed in the USA
LVHW100747251022
731430LV00004B/183